PLOT AND BOTHERED

NEVERMORE BOOKSHOP MYSTERIES, BOOK 9

STEFFANIE HOLMES

BACCHANALIA HOUSE

PLOT AND BOTHERED

Wedding bells are ringing at Nevermore Bookshop!

Mina, Heathcliff, Morrie, and Quoth are tying the knot in an extravagant ceremony. But when someone sabotages the decorations and Heathcliff receives a threatening note, they realise that a saboteur in the village doesn't want them to have their happily-ever-after.

Their wedding misadventures turn deadly when the wedding saboteur murders the celebrant.

Add in a duck-napping, disastrous dance lessons, absent book reviewers, Mina's mother's newest business venture, and visits from old friends…and enemies, and Mina has a matrimonial catastrophe on her hands.

Will she make it down the aisle to marry her fictional men, or does someone intend the wedding toast to be, "eat, drink, and be murdered?"

Will our foursome be able to tie the knot amongst the chaos and carnage? Find out in the final book in the Nevermore Bookshop Mysteries – *Plot and Bothered.*

JOIN THE NEWSLETTER FOR UPDATES

Want a free bonus scene from Quoth's point of view? Grab a free copy of *Cabinet of Curiosities* – a Steffanie Holmes compendium of short stories and bonus scenes – when you sign up for updates with the Steffanie Holmes newsletter.

www.steffanieholmes.com/newsletter

Every week in my newsletter I talk about the true-life hauntings, strange happenings, crumbling ruins, and creepy facts that inspire my stories. You'll also get newsletter-exclusive bonus scenes and updates. I love to talk to my readers, so come join us for some spooky fun :)

Welcome to
Argleton Village
Population: 2,265…
… and shrinking
LACHLAN HALL
ROSE & WIMPLE
NEVERMORE
BOOKSHOP
BAKERY
VILLAGE GREEN
MRS ELLIS' HOUSE
NEW RAILWAY
STATION
KING'S COPSE WOOD
POLICE STATION
OLD RAILWAY
STATION

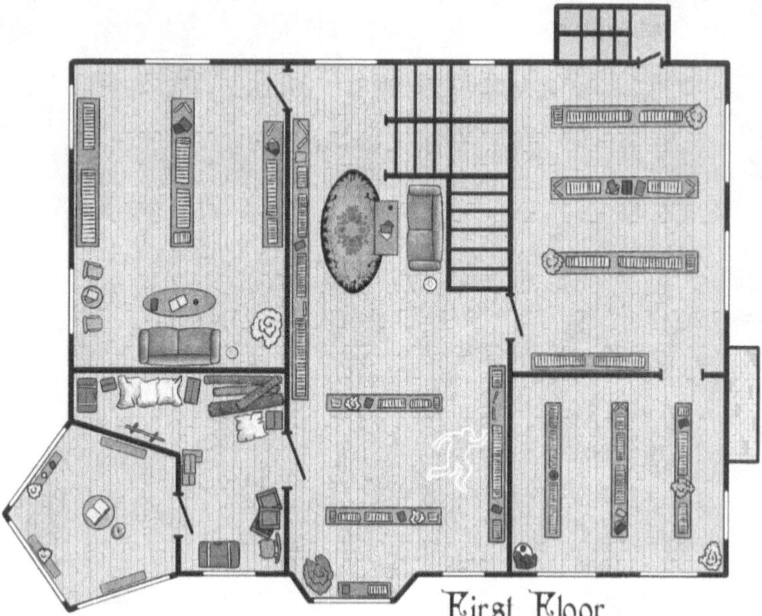

First Floor

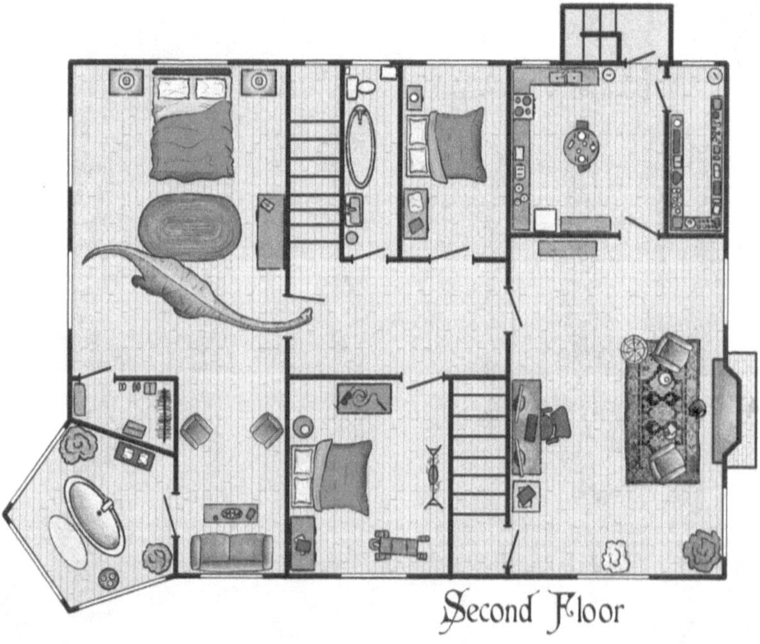

Second Floor

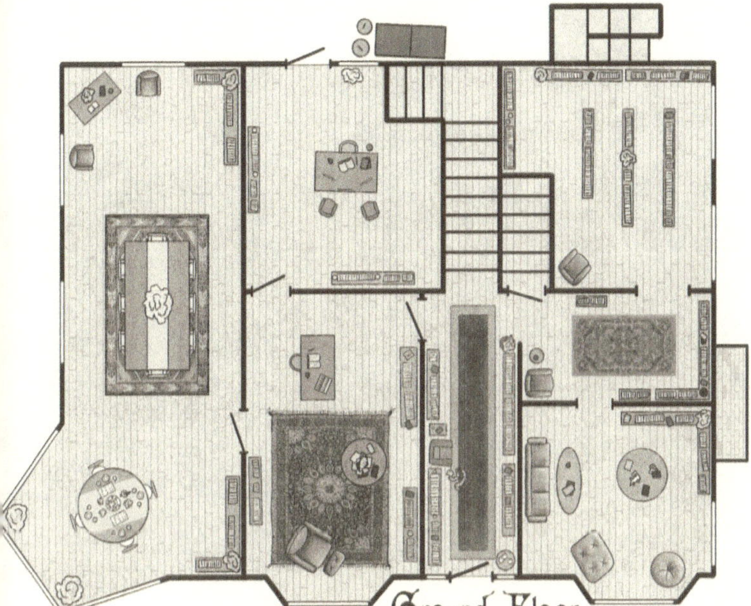

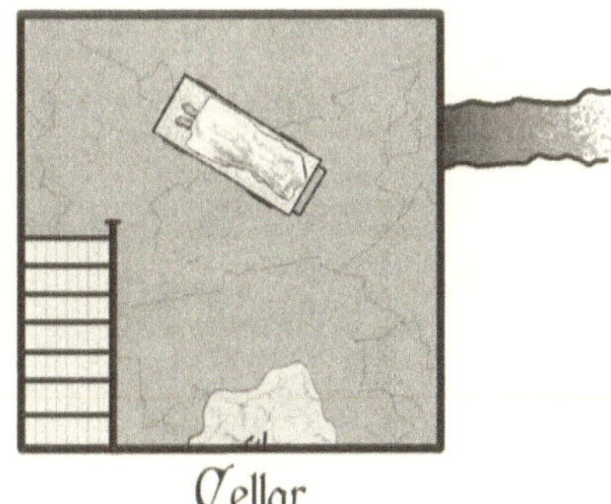

Ground Floor

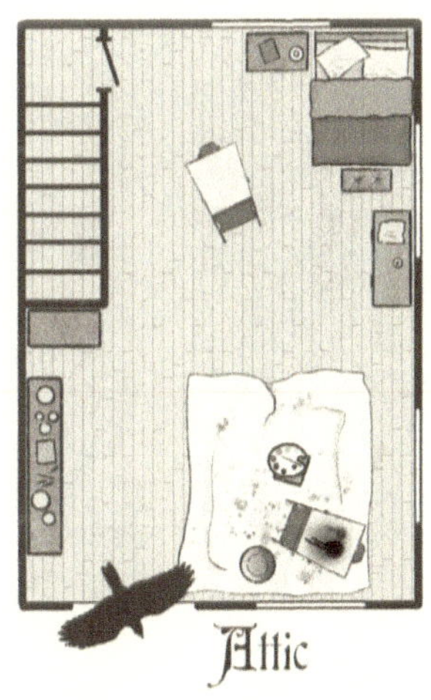

Attic

Cellar

*To the 57 cups of tea that got me through writing this manuscript,
and the hot husband who fetched them for me.
Mmmmm, tea.*

Reader, I married him.

–Charlotte Brontë, Jane Eyre

ANNOUNCEMENT TAPED TO DOOR OF NEVERMORE BOOKSHOP

Dear customers,

Nevermore Bookshop is closed ~~forever~~ for the next two weeks because Mina, Heathcliff, Morrie, and Allan are getting married!

We'll see you ~~never again please go away~~ at the ceremony at Lachlan Hall on the 20th, and then at the launch of Mina's debut novel, *A Dead And Stormy Night*, at Nevermore Bookshop on the 21st! It's going to be a grand affair, with a London photographer and plenty of literary superstars in attendance.

If you need to get in touch with Heathcliff about wedding plans, don't.

If you need to get in touch with Mina about book launch business, then please go across the street to her office in Nevermore Gallery and sneak up on her. She loves that.

CHAPTER 1
MINA

"— A dangerous criminal escaped from the nearby Crixley Institution. Please be on the lookout for a—"

"Can we turn that down?" I jerked my head up from behind my computer screen and yelled in the vague direction of the downstairs studio.

"—in other local news, a brand new fashion exhibition is coming to the Crookshollow Museum, featuring some of the hottest designers of the last decade, and the neighborhood feud over a pet duck reaches new heights as—

"What's that?" Quoth yelled back. "You want us to put on some Motown?"

"—And now, for the weather, this cold front we've been monitoring looks to be closing in, which means that we could be in for a wet week ahead—"

"No Motown." I deleted the email address I'd written incorrectly for the third time. "I just want you to turn the volume down—"

The door to my office flung open all the way. Oscar lifted his head from my foot as Morrie poked his around the corner. "Gorgeous, I heard you yelling about how much you hate clowns. Is a clown bothering you? Is one of those sadistic, rouged, banana-foot flamingos keeping you from your work? Fear not, because I'm here to help. I'll make certain no clown ever darkens your doorstep again—"

"You don't need to go on a clown-murdering spree," I sighed. "I just want you guys to turn the radio down. I can't concentrate with all the noise."

"Oh, sorry." Morrie frowned. "It's just that Smooth Loamshire is giving away a lifetime supply of cheesecakes to the first caller who hears the magic sound, and I was hoping to win it for the wedding. I know how much you love cheesecake."

He's...what?

I rested my elbows on my desk and glared in the vague direction of the Napoleon of Crime. "Heathcliff already has Oliver baking round the clock on some elaborate dessert concoction that I'm not allowed to know anything about. I don't think we *need* a lifetime supply of cheesecake."

Even with my poor eyesight, I could tell Morrie was making his pouting face. "If you recall, *you* insisted we invite the whole village to this shindig. Never underestimate the abilities of a horde of polite British party guests to decimate the dessert buffet. I'm simply being pragmatic."

"Fine, but you're the world's foremost criminal master-mind, in possession of deep coffers filled with ill-gotten gains. Surely you can purchase your own cheesecakes?"

"That's not the point. I'm trying to be *romantic*." Morrie pouted. "Heathcliff gets to plan a whole wedding for you. Quoth's downstairs creating yet another artistic masterpiece that will have you swooning. All I'm allowed to do is show up and look pretty, which granted, is a job to which I am particu-larly well-suited, but I'd like to swoop in as the cheesecake-supplying hero, or some other hero who will romantically save the day and have you kneeling at my feet—"

"Luckily, I have just the job for you. Can you *romantically* turn the volume down?" I peered over my computer screen and the piles of embossed paper my Braille printer was still spitting out. "I've got the last of my press invites to send out, and then I have to get the edited manuscript to Jerry over at Argleton Print or he won't be able to print enough copies in time for the launch party."

I ran my fingers along my Braille display, checking over the text of my email for what must have been the thirtieth time. I'd been training for months on using a screen reader – software on my phone and laptop that figured out what was on screen and allowed me to use keyboard commands to navigate and do pretty much anything a sighted person could do. Usually, I had the screen reader read out what was on screen, but when I was working on my book, I preferred to use the Braille display. When the computer reads to you, it doesn't pick out when you drop an apostrophe or use here instead of hair. But with the Braille display, I could check every word, phrase, and sentence with my fingers to make sure that they were perfect.

I needed everything about this book to be *perfect*.

I'd spent the last two months since I got back from the Meddleworth Writers Retreat (where I didn't do much writing but we *did* solve a doozy of a murder) holed up in this room for nine hours a day, frantically polishing my debut novel. I'd written a fictionalized version of what happened to me over the last two years – getting fired from my dream fashion job, returning to the small English village where I'd grown up, getting a job in a magical bookshop, solving a murder (or eight), finding out that I'm the daughter of the blind poet Homer, slaying literature's most infamous vampire, and falling in love with Heathcliff Earnshaw, James Moriarty, and Quoth the raven.

Even without my fictional embellishments, the story would

never pass for a biography. Which was probably just as well that I was publishing it under a pseudonym, since I'd filled it with loads of smut. Hey, sex sells, right?

I wanted my book to help people heal after a setback. And all romance readers understand the healing powers of multiple orgasms.

I'd come to Nevermore Bookshop broken and lonely. I thought my diagnosis meant that my life was over. Instead, I stumbled into adventures I never imagined possible, and I fell in love with three beautiful, impossible men, and somehow (partially through the healing power of great cock), I learned to love myself again.

I realized that my disability was part of me, but it didn't have to *define* me.

Now, I was ready to share that story with the world. And hopefully, make some money.

Owning a bookshop that's forced to compete against The-Store-That-Shall-Not-Be-Named wasn't exactly a road to riches, and I had bills to pay and guide dog food to purchase and a grandmother cat with six baby kittens who needed to be kept in the lifestyle to which they'd become accustomed.

I didn't just want to write a book, I wanted a *career* where my creative spirit could thrive, like the career in fashion I'd given up when I started losing my sight.

I decided to self-publish my book after my writing friend Christina showed me how she uploaded hers to The-Store-That-Shall-Not-Be-Named, created a paperback that prints on demand whenever someone orders it, and arranged for all her fancy London literary friends to blurb and review it. She was doing really well, and I was hoping a little bit of her magic would rub off on me.

Which was why I was trying to organize the biggest book launch that Nevermore Bookshop had ever seen.

The evening after my wedding.

Because I was *bonkers*.

Originally, the wedding and book launch were going to be a month apart, but Heathcliff had some issues with our original venue and Cynthia offered us Lachlan Hall, but only if we could do it the day before the book launch.

When Heathcliff first suggested the idea, I thought it would be a fun way to extend the celebrations and enable our out-of-town friends to attend both events if they wanted.

Reader, I was wrong.

Launching your debut novel a day after your wedding was *not* fun, especially when I'd been inviting publishers, reviewers, and every bookish person I knew for *weeks* and they were all ignoring me.

I thought that with the connections I'd made at Meddleworth and from bookselling, and our modest following online (I'd made some videos of Quoth hopping along the bookshelves and Oscar helping me put books away, and they'd gone semi-viral), people would be interested in my book.

But so far, with the exception of my friends in the village, Morrie's ex-boyfriend Sherlock, and the Argleton Spirit Seekers Society, I hadn't got a *single* RSVP. And it was starting to freak me out.

—join us on Smooth Loamshire for an hour of non-stop country and western classics. Yee-haw!

"Morrie, the radio." I shot Morrie my best blind-girl glare. "*Please.*"

"Since you asked so nicely."

Morrie snapped out his foot and, with the precision of a mathematician who's trained in the martial arts since childhood, slammed the door shut.

I swallowed.

"That's not what I meant," I said, but my mouth had gone

dry. Tension crackled between us, as it always did when Morrie walked that tightrope between his need to control everything and the dark chaos of his psyche. "I have to finish these emails, and proofread my manuscript, and..."

"And?"

"Uh." I forgot what else I had to do. Morrie had that effect on me.

Morrie regarded the pile of Braille pages on my desk with a smirk that I could sense even when I couldn't actually see it. "I thought you finished proofreading the manuscript last month."

"Yes, but then I randomly opened it to page 23 and discovered I'd used a semicolon instead of a colon, and now I'm doubting everything."

Morrie leaned over the desk and cupped the back of my neck, pulling me out of my seat and across the desk until our lips were an inch apart. Every atom of me sizzled with anticipation, trapped in the web that only James Moriarty could spin.

The purr of his voice rumbled through my body, stoking an ache deep in my belly. "My little perfectionist. Do you know what I think these pages need?"

"Is it a fancypants London reviewer, publishing executive, or paper to review them? Because you'd be right."

"I think they need you spread out over them, coming around my cock like a good girl."

"Morrie..." I sighed but knew I couldn't fight him as his breath trailed down my neck and to my collarbone. He wasn't even *touching* me and I was already a quivering mess.

"We shouldn't do this. I don't have *time*. The book launch is in five days," I managed to breathe out as his lips finally met my skin, kissing the spot on my collarbone that lit my body on fire.

"If that's how you really feel," he whispered into my skin, "I'll let you get back to work."

Morrie drew back sharply.

By Isis.

I whimpered involuntarily, already missing his touch.

"What—" but I didn't get a chance to finish the sentence before I felt him come up behind me, his hips trapping mine against the edge of the desk, his body caging me in.

I closed my eyes, blocking out the light and just feeling each new sensation as his hands roamed over my body. My skin prickled everywhere his expert hands touched, even through my clothes.

He slid down my body, kneeling behind the desk. I heard Oscar whimper as he retreated into the corner behind the desk, so his poor innocent doggie eyes wouldn't be assaulted by whatever Morrie intended to do. There was a light tap at my ankles, then an abrupt push when I didn't comply, shoving my legs wide.

"Morrie, what are you doing?" I managed to ask between deep breaths.

"Letting you work, gorgeous. Go on, keep doing what you're doing."

I snorted. "How am I supposed to do that when you're down there, doing whatever *you're* doing?"

He laughed that cruel, arrogant laugh of his, the one that utterly disintegrated my self-control as the vibrations tickled my bare skin where my skirt met my thighs.

"That's not my problem, gorgeous. I never said that I wouldn't be a distraction." His kisses trailed up my leg as his strong hands pushed my legs wider, giving him better access to my body.

Morrie pressed a hand into the small of my back, bending me over the desk and giving him better access to what he was wanting.

His lips skirted over my panties, driving me absolutely wild. I pressed my cheek against a stack of pages, knowing I was probably flattening the dots so I wouldn't be able to read them later, but I didn't care.

Morrie breathed heavily before he pushed aside the fabric with his deft fingers and let the pad of his thumb roam over my lips.

"If your book launch is in five days, that means that in four days, you're going to be my wife."

"Morrie," I gasped as his finger circled me.

"I love it when you say my name," he whispered, his breath caressing me. "And soon, Mina Wilde, all of this will be *mine*."

He slid his finger inside me, stroking in a slow, languid rhythm.

"Not just yours," I managed to choke out.

"No, not just mine. *Ours*. Mine and Heathcliff's and Quoth's. You'll be shackling yourself to three nefarious villains forever. But judging by how wet you are, I don't think you mind at all. They say that it's bad luck to defile the bride before the wedding night, but I've never been one for obeying the rules."

He dived his tongue inside me.

I gasped at the new sensation, gripping the desk to keep my balance. His tongue pressed needfully against me. My nipples pressed against the Braille paper, hard as pebbles through my shirt.

"Yes," Morrie murmured against me. "I think you'll make a lovely wife, Mina Wilde."

My skin prickled as he lapped up every drop of me, taking his sweet, deliberate time. He added his fingers to spread me further as he thrust his expert tongue in and out of me before dragging it up to circle my clit.

"Morrie, I'm so close," I gasped, leaning forward, the rough dots of the Braille paper brushing against my cheek. I slid my arm out to grip the other edge, sending a pile of pages cascading to the floor.

It would probably take me hours to get everything back in order. A few minutes ago, I would have been panicking about it, but as fireworks rippled through my core and stars burst behind my closed eyelids, that was the last thing on my mind as I cried out my orgasm, riding it on Morrie's expert tongue.

"Do you want more distracting?" he growled, sinking his teeth lightly into the flesh of my ass while his fingers built me up again with slow thrusts.

"Yes, please," I begged, pushing my hips forward to meet his awaiting thrusts.

Morrie laughed as his tongue plunged back inside me, matching the push and pull of his fingers.

He drove me senseless with this onslaught. The whole world collapsed into a pinprick, nothing existing anymore outside of the pleasure he offered me. My next climax was hard and fast, bursts of light shooting through me as my whole body shook. More Braille pages tumbled off the desk.

Before I could even come down from my high, Morrie was up and his strong body behind me, holding me in place as I slumped over the desk, my skirt now wrapped around my waist.

A dopey smile crossed my face as I laid my cheek back down on the Braille pages, knowing that my skin would bear the imprint of all the raised dots. Morrie slapped my ass playfully, making me yelp, before he gripped my hips and entered me in one long thrust.

Just like his tongue, he moved with a cool, controlled manner that had my knees buckling, and I was glad I had the desk to grab onto as he impaled me with his monstrous cock.

"Are you going to come for me again, gorgeous? Are you going to scream my name as you come all over my cock? Are you going to make Quoth downstairs jealous that he's not up here distracting you, too?"

"Yes, yes," I moaned, pushing my ass back against him, sending another avalanche of paper falling to the floor.

Damn, how many of those sheets were there?

I was quickly drawn back to the moment by the build-up of pleasure pooling between my thighs. The sheer size of Morrie stole the breath from my lungs, and when he worked his way inside me with that insouciant arrogance of his, as if being spread out beneath him was what I'd been asking for all along, I became a *mess*.

By Hathor, but Morrie is good at getting me out of my own head.

"That's it, gorgeous. Come for me, my future wife. Let me hear you scream my name." Morrie thrust harder as he reached between my legs, circling my wet clit with his fingers.

He groaned again, the sound absolutely *feral*, and I knew with shuddering certainty that the last vestiges of his well-honed control had finally snapped. When he drove into me again, it was with such force that the desk creaked and slid across the floor.

"Mina." His hips thrust as his voice rumbled inside my chest. His scent swirled around me, that familiar grapefruit and vanilla aftershave that belied his villainous nature.

I answered with an incoherent moan that might've been his name and might've been my shopping list, but it didn't matter when I writhed beneath him, pinned to the desk by his strong hands and the relentless pace of his hips.

"Morrie," I moaned again, riding his touch as the electricity hit me fast and hard like a bolt of lightning. This time, when my orgasm hit, I didn't try to hold back, and rode the wave hard, screaming out Morrie's name as I let my body spasm beneath his.

"Fuck, Mina," he growled, pushing harder, gripping my waist as I felt him release the final flimsy thread of his control.

I tried to steady my breathing as I collapsed back onto the

desk. Morrie stayed inside me for a moment longer, leaning over to lay a trail of kisses down my skin before pulling out.

Morrie lay down, resting his cheek on the desk beside me, crushing more Braille dots. His vanilla and grapefruit scent wafted around me, and I found myself relaxing. He reached over, digging his long, expert fingers into the knots in my shoulders.

I wanted to protest and tell him I had so much more work to do, but as my thighs still tingled and the tension in my shoulders fell away, I knew there was no way I could say no to a bit of pampering.

The book could wait just a little longer.

"Listen to me, gorgeous. So what if none of those publishing bigwigs show up. Everyone who matters to you is going to love your book. You shouldn't be worrying about this now," he murmured as his fingers dug into a particularly stubborn knot.

Maybe he's right. So what if no one came to my book launch? It didn't matter. In four days, I was marrying three of literature's greatest villains, who I loved more than I'd love a Henry Rollins-era Black Flag reunion tour, and nothing else mattered—

DING.

That's an email!

"Leave it, gorgeous, we're snuggling," Morrie groaned.

But I'd already rolled over and was frantically searching for my phone. My fingers grazed it, right on the edge of the table. I picked it up and clicked on the email sender.

My phone read out the sender's name. "Jen Whately."

The Jen Whately.

My heart pounded against my ribs. Jen was the editorial director at my *dream* publishing house and a friend of Christina Olivian. I'd met her six months ago when Christina brought her into Nevermore to search for a first-edition Oscar Wilde as a gift for a friend.

After I picked my jaw up off the ground, we got to chatting. Jen gave me her card. We'd been emailing back and forth a bit after I tracked down that Oscar Wilde for her. I'd sent her an invite and an advance copy of the book, and I knew it was a long shot, but I'd been secretly hoping that she'd love my book so much that she'd want to pick it up for publication, maybe a print-only deal where I got to publish the ebook but they made one of those pretty gilded-edge special editions...

"Who is that, gorgeous?" Morrie's hands roamed over the curve of my ass.

"Jen Whately. The publisher I was telling you about. The one I was hoping..."

I nearly dropped my phone.

Morrie sat up, instantly interested. "Go on, read it out. I want to hear how brilliant she thinks you are and how many zeroes are on the end of the cheque she's offering you for your brilliant, smutty book."

With trembling hands, I clicked on the email. My phone started to read out Jan's reply:

Mina,

Thank you very much for the invite. I'm a big fan of your little bookshop, so I'm going to give you some advice that I don't give freely to the gazillion other aspiring writers who contact me. First, you're self-publishing your book, which isn't looked upon favorably in my industry. Second, making your heroine blind is going to be a hard sell. Readers want to feel as though they relate to a heroine, and they won't be able to if she can't see. I'm sorry, I know this isn't what you want to hear.

Write something more commercial, or rewrite this book without the blindness, and I'll happily look at it.

> *I wish you all the best, and I hope to return to your charming
> store when I'm next in the area.*
>
> *Yours, Jen*

My heart thudded against my chest. *People can't relate to my heroine?* But...

I wanted to argue. I wanted to scream that people seemed to relate to me just fine.

I wanted to explain how desperately I needed to read a story like this when I first got my diagnosis.

But there was no point.

Jen knew best. She was the publishing expert.

She knows what she's talking about. If she says that my book isn't commercial enough, then...

Morrie grabbed my phone from my hands and scanned the email. "I cannot believe she said that to you. I hope this woman enjoys one-of-a-kind designer accessories, because I'm going to weave her intestines into an elegant evening purse."

I squeezed my eyes shut. *Astarte, don't let me start crying in front of him.* "Morrie, don't make a big deal about it. *Please.*"

"I'm going to string her teeth onto a necklace and knit her eyebrows into a winter coat—"

"How would you even get enough fibre from eyebrows for— never mind. Morrie—"

"Mina, she said that people can't relate to your story. *Can't relate to your story.* Everyone in the world can relate to the story of having to find yourself again after a setback. Everyone except me, that is, because I've never experienced a setback in my life."

"It's fine." I snatched my phone from him and shoved it back into my pocket. As I straightened my skirt, I swallowed down the hurt until it was deep inside me. "Jen knows this industry. If she doesn't think it's relatable, she's probably right. It explains why no one's returned my emails."

"Mina, don't—"

"I'm fine with it, *really*. It's a quirky little book. I shouldn't expect so much. Even if no one comes to the book launch, the four of us and the Spirit Seekers Society will still have an amazing time." I forced a smile. "And look on the bright side, this way we'll know there will definitely be enough sausage rolls."

I looked away from him, frantically trying to blink back the tears. I didn't want to cry four days before my wedding day.

I've made a huge mistake.

I worked so hard on this book. I poured everything I had into it. All my friends who read it said that it's a fun story. I guess I'd been cocooned within their praise for so long that I was so sure people would love it, that if I could just get the word out, I'd find an audience who wanted to read about a heroine who fell into a magical bookshop, solved murders, and fell in love with three fictional men.

But clearly, I was wrong.

"You sound so disappointed—"

"I'm fine!" I bent over my laptop again, typing random gibberish on the screen. "Now, I've got a ton of work to do and only days to do it in, so can you please go downstairs and tell Quoth to turn down the radio?"

CHAPTER 2
MORRIE

I rubbed my hands together as I emerged from Mina's office. She gave me a faint wave from behind her phone screen, her hair mussed around her face and her gorgeous green eyes all blown out from the orgasms I gave her. She was already re-reading that email.

I longed to reach into the screen and do something rather unsavory to this Jen Whately. How could she say that to Mina? How could she think that no one could relate to Mina's story?

Mina had overcome challenges. She'd used her brain and her creativity to get us out of many sticky spots. She'd been at knife-point, gun-point, garrote-point, and still she believed the best in people. She touched the hearts of every person in this village. She'd worked alongside Heathcliff for over a year without once cowering in fear.

She defeated a centuries-old fictional *vampire*.

She changed *me*, a feat I'd never have thought possible.

I used to be an uncaring, unfeeling criminal mastermind who hid myself behind a mask and a wicked tongue, until she split me open and forced all my darkest secrets to spill out.

I'm *still* a criminal mastermind, but I am so much more

powerful now that I have a family – a real family – to care about and protect.

How was that not relatable?

I knew Mina too well to believe that she'd forget about that email. She was stewing over Jen's words right now, her beautiful features all twisted up with worry. I wanted to make it better, but barring my idea to transform various parts of Jen's anatomy into wearable accessories, I didn't know how. And unfortunately, I had to get back downstairs.

My visit to her office wasn't for selfish reasons – I was on a mission.

I stole back downstairs, past Quoth who was rushing around the communal art studio, singing along to a Taylor Swift song on the radio as he picked up drop cloths and slotted paintbrushes back into their cubbies. He'd tied his silken hair back off his face at the nape of his neck by a scrap of velvet ribbon, and despite his frenzied movements, his fire-rimmed eyes were serene.

Quoth was never happier than when he was doing something disgustingly thoughtful for Mina or working on his art, and our current project combined both his talents.

Relief swept over me to see the large space in the corner of the studio that had for the past three weeks been occupied by something large and ungainly hidden beneath a black cloth. *The mission was a success.*

I leaned over and flicked off the radio. Quoth continued singing, not even noticing that the music had stopped.

My pulse quickened as my eyes darted around the Nevermore Gallery, searching for the mastermind behind today's shenanigans.

There he was. Leaning against the doorframe, rubbing his muscled arms and looking every bit like he'd just maneuvered said ungainly object through narrow Butcher Street to the waiting truck, was Heathcliff.

A familiar butterfly flapped its wings inside my chest as I approached him. Mina Wilde was the love of my life, the woman I would burn the world for, but this man also held a special piece of my black heart in his thick fist, and he squeezed so tight that his love made me struggle for air.

I'd been living with Heathcliff Earnshaw for years, and still, the sight of him majestic in his wrath made me recall the first day I entered Nevermore Bookshop and met my villainous match. I'd had many men in my bed over the years, men who fell to their knees to worship me, but Heathcliff was the only man I'd ever kneel for.

But I never dreamed that he felt anything for me other than annoyance.

All we'd needed to close the chasm between us into a debaucherous entanglement was Mina Wilde breaking open our hearts and laying bare our every hidden desire.

Worth it.

I sidled up to him and leaned in close, my lips brushing the stubble where he'd attempted to trim his unruly beard. "You did it?"

He grunted in reply.

I leaned back and placed my hand to my ear. "What was that? 'Why, *thank you,* Morrie, for brilliantly distracting Mina with your wicked tongue and impressive cock so I could sneak Quoth's photo booth down Butcher Street and onto the back of Jo's new pickup.' Oh, 'tis nothing, really. I can't help my altruistic heart. Someone had to take one for the team—"

He glowered at me. "Yes, altruism. That's the reason you volunteered to be the distraction while I dragged a half-ton monstrosity up the hill and loaded it onto the bed of the pickup *by myself.*"

"You had Quoth."

Quoth shot me a look over his shoulder that said, *please don't bring me into this.*

Heathcliff snorted. "Some help he was. He saw Dorothy Ingram strolling across the green and got all feathery, didn't he? He would've smashed his corner on the stone wall if I hadn't taken all the weight."

"Did she see you?" I asked.

"Mina? I bloody hope not. That's what your wicked tongue was for, to make sure that she didn't happen to look out the window at the exact wrong time, just when the light was enough for her to see—"

"I made certain our girl wasn't anywhere near the window." I grinned, my cock dancing a little jig at the memory of having her bent over her desk. "I was referring to our favorite village sourpuss."

"Thankfully, Dorothy Ingram had those beady eyes of hers fixed on some teenagers loitering outside the pub. I got the thing tied down without her seeing it, and now I'm going to need surgery to fix my busted shoulders." Heathcliff's dark eyes searched out Quoth, who was cowering behind a desk. "You owe me, birdie. You'd better have some Scotch stashed somewhere in the gallery."

Quoth scurried away to fetch Heathcliff his medicine. Heathcliff slid onto the paint-splattered leather sofa under the window and wiped the sweat from his brow. He looked more harried than I'd ever seen him, which was unusual considering that Nevermore was temporarily closed and he hadn't had to deal with customers for a week.

After Dorothy Ingram chased us away from our first wedding venue of the town hall, Mina's friend and fellow member of the Spirit Seekers Society, Cynthia Lachlan, offered to host the wedding for us at Lachlan Hall at no charge. Cynthia is yet another person who owes a debt to Mina, as our girl saved her from being blamed for several murders of Banned Book Club members, caught a killer at her Jane Austen Experience weekend, and then rescued her ex-husband Grey from the clutches of Dracula.

The only problem was that Lachlan Hall was booked solid with events, and Cynthia had only one day when she could fit us in between the end of the British Heritage tour season and before a crew of stonemasons moved in to start repairs to the east turret. And that day just happened to be one night before Mina's book launch.

Mina wanted to have all our friends in the village for both events, so we decided to go for it. Even my ex Sherlock was coming down from London for the occasion. But it meant that Mina wouldn't have time to organize the wedding on top of the book launch, and it was outdated and sexist to assume that the woman was the one in a relationship who would plan a wedding. For three villains conceived by Victorian white male writers, we are the epitome of modern feminists.

I assumed that Mina planned to ask me to take over wedding planning since I'm used to forcing minions to do my bidding. Or she would perhaps choose Quoth, who has an artistic eye.

But Mina asked Heathcliff. Or he volunteered. I couldn't actually remember. But somehow, literature's great gothic anti-hero, a man who loathed people and fuss and everything about weddings except for the vows and the open bar, had turned his obsessive nature to the world of table runners and invitation fonts.

Truthfully, he'd proven surprisingly good at pulling together a decadent, book-themed wedding in a few short months. One glower from Heathcliff and the vendors caved to his every whim.

And he had many whims.

Such as today's shenanigans. Because we were having the wedding in a bonafide castle, Heathcliff decided that he was going to try to recreate scenes from one of Mina's favorite Disney movies, *Beauty and the Beast.* She often said that Beast giving Belle a library was one of the most romantic things that she'd ever seen.

So Heathcliff had this idea to transform the Lachlan Hall library into the library from the movie for our photos. He asked Quoth to help him make props, and our birdie went a bit overboard.

Quoth constructed an enormous faux fireplace that exactly matched the one in the movie. That's what we'd transported today, as well as models of the inanimate object characters enchanted to speak, and a large trompe-l'œil that would hang on the ceiling to make the library appear four storeys high instead of *merely* two, all of them bedecked with fairy lights and sparkle so that Mina could see them.

Mina would *flip* when we unveiled the library. Provided all of Quoth's sculptures made it to the venue in one piece. This was why Heathcliff wanted the two of us to join him at Lachlan Hall now, while they were installed, to ensure everything went perfectly.

Heathcliff glared at his watch. "We'd better get going. I need to chat with Cynthia about the floral arrangements before we arrange the Disney sculptures."

"There's a sentence I never dreamed I'd hear you utter."

"Can you make that smart mouth of yours useful and call the birdie? He seems to have disappeared." Heathcliff winced as he rolled his shoulders.

"Quoth?" I headed into the back room, where Quoth had gone to wash his hands but had become distracted by a library-themed seating chart poster. "Birdie, Sir Snarkleton of Snozzberry wants to leave now."

"Oh, sorry." Quoth tossed his brushes into water and packed away the seating chart into a corner of the studio so that Mina wouldn't accidentally find it. He was going all out on the wedding prep, just like Heathcliff, and he even had his art students working around the clock on the various installations.

If I was being bitterly honest, all their activity made me feel a bit...superfluous. This was not a feeling I was accustomed to... well, apart from that unfortunate episode some months back when I had to go into hiding with my ex-boyfriend, but that ugliness was behind us.

Still, I wished I had more to contribute to Mina's surprise wedding than my beautiful body.

Quoth seemed to sense my unease, because he raised his head, his orange-rimmed eyes meeting mine. "You are needed, Morrie. Always."

"I never doubted it."

"Good. Because right now, I need you to pick up my clothes for me." He smiled that genuine Quoth smile and forced his shift. Before my eyes, he shrunk into his clothing, his face contorting as his nose and mouth became a beak, his spine and ribs twisting as he unfurled his arms into sleek black wings.

Quoth flapped twice to dislodge the sleeve of his shirt from his wingtip, then flew over to perch on my shoulder, leaving a pile of paint-splattered clothes on the floor.

I picked up his clothing and folded it neatly on a chair, then called an Uber to take us to Lachlan Hall. (If I'm being factual, I called *two* Ubers, because the first one refused to allow a raven in the car. Heathcliff thumped on the window as the driver pulled away in a hurry. "This is discrimination! He's my emotional support raven!")

Given how tightly wound Heathcliff was over the wedding, that felt accurate.

"Croak." Quoth hopped over the back of my seat and nipped Heathcliff on the ear – a corvid attempt to calm him down. It had the opposite effect, causing Heathcliff to yelp and drop his phone between the seats, which made his face go redder than I'd ever seen it.

Heathcliff was a ball of nerves as we pulled up to Lachlan Hall.

The stately home was buzzing with people. This was why Quoth didn't want to attend in his human form. Two men shoved past us on the steps, carrying a heavy oak table. A woman nearly brained me with an armload of crockery, and someone driving a golf cart stacked with wine glasses saw Heathcliff and hastily performed a U-turn to flee in the opposite direction. I caught a glimpse of their face, and felt a twang of familiarity, but I couldn't place them.

Not all of these people were for our wedding, surely? Cynthia was hosting a National Trust conference this week, but that was mostly in the orangery...

Heathcliff nearly bowled over the butler as he stormed inside. Luckily, Iwan Carew poked his head out of a reception room, stopping the two of us in our tracks with his disarmingly genuine smile.

"Heathcliff, my friend." Iwan wrapped his arms around Heathcliff's shoulders, taking his life into his hands. "How are you, mate? Excited about the big day?"

Heathcliff's mouth started to twist up into his signature scowl, but it didn't quite reach its destination. Iwan's infectious personality had disarmed even Sir Snarkypuss.

Heathcliff had gone to every local celebrant in the area to find someone to officiate our unconventional wedding. In England, our ceremony wouldn't be legally binding, but it was common for couples to hire a celebrant to perform their wedding ceremony and then to go to the registry office and have a registrar do the legal stuff later, so we figured we'd just do that sans legal nonsense.

However, what we hadn't counted on was Dorothy Ingram's campaign against our nuptials. She was so convinced that her god cared enough that Mina was fake-marrying three men that she'd got in the ear of every celebrant within a thirty-mile radius and ensured they knew that if they married us, they'd receive so many complaints that they'd never perform another wedding ceremony again.

But when Heathcliff found Iwan, the Welsh celebrant had smiled his huge, friendly grin at Heathcliff and told him that this wasn't his first encounter with Dorothy Ingram. She'd come after him for his campaigning for gay marriage before it was made legal in 2013. "I wasn't afraid of her then, and I'm not afraid of her now. If the four of you are madly in love and you want to make it official and have a smashing good party, I'm honored to be part of that. And I want to help with the planning, too. I happen to be Loamshire's most sought-after wedding stylist."

So Iwan became our new favorite person. He was a font of wedding knowledge and had basically moved into Lachlan Hall to help with the last-minute plans. In Mina's absence, he'd kept Heathcliff's head from rolling off his shoulders.

"I'll be excited once I know that everything is perfect," Heathcliff muttered, drawing back slowly, his eyes darting around nervously. "Did Jo arrive with the fireplace prop?"

"She's around back unloading it now." Iwan patted Quoth on the top of his head, then waved us deeper into the house. "And the flower samples came, but they were terrible, so I sent them back. New ones will arrive tomorrow, and they *will* be perfect. Some bastard stole the wait staff's uniforms, but I've ordered more, because if we have naked waitstaff it will be quite a different event! And Oliver sent over two cake options to choose from, and I told him that *of course* Mina is a triple chocolate raspberry girl—"

Of course, Quoth said inside my head as we followed Iwan through the ornate foyer toward the ballroom, where the ceremony would be held. We were just about to step inside when Cynthia Lachlan burst through the double doors, nearly bowling us over.

"Oh, Morrie, Heathcliff, bird, it's lovely to see you again." Cynthia's over-lipsticked mouth curved downward. "I'm afraid I have some distressing news."

Heathcliff froze. "What?"

"Don't look so terrified. I'm certain that it's nothing, but, Iwan, could you liaise with the event staff while I talk to them about our little issue..."

"Of course." Iwan gave a jaunty bow. "Don't worry, friends. This is a minor setback. Everything will be perfect for your wedding!"

"What minor setback?" Heathcliff looked ready to explode.

"It's all rather odd." Cynthia led us into a drawing room, where several boxes had been scattered across the furniture. "This morning I took delivery of the chair covers."

That's right. Quoth hopped excitedly on my shoulder. *Iwan and I decided on blood-red chair covers with contrasting gold bows so that Mina could see the contrast and—*

Cynthia upended one of the boxes. Ribbons of torn red and gold fabric tumbled out, like blood and glitter.

"This is a rather avant-garde interpretation of chair 'cover'," I said.

Heathcliff's mouth hung open. "What happened..."

Cynthia picked up a scrap of fabric between her fingers and pinched her face, as if the ruined fabric offended her every sense. "This is how they arrived. Every single box is the same. I called the company and gave them an earful. According to them, they delivered the order yesterday, not today, and they said that someone at the house checked and signed for them. I don't understand how this could have happened! They've also told me that they won't have time to remake the order before the wedding. I'm so sorry."

Heathcliff dug his hand into the pile of scraps, his face scarlet with rage. "Someone's head will roll for this."

"It gets worse." Cynthia pushed a folded piece of paper into his hands. "I found this sitting on top of the first box."

I peered over his shoulder as Heathcliff unfolded the paper. Letters cut from magazines were glued onto a sheet of printer paper, like an old-school ransom note. (I'd seen a few like this in my lifetime, although I've never personally sent one. Arts and crafts weren't my forte, and when James Moriarty sends a ransom note, he handwrites it and signs his name. A criminal should have a little class.)

The note read:

MINA WILDE, YOU DON'T DESERVE TO BE HAPPY.
I'M HERE TO RUIN YOUR WEDDING.
BY ANY MEANS NECESSARY.

NOTICE NAILED TO THE DOOR OF ARGLETON PRESBYTERIAN CHURCH

Sinners in our midst! Pray for Argleton!

Notice from the Argleton Defense against Immorality, Adultery, Bestiality, Lucifer and the Occult group.

It has come to our attention that the inhabitants of Nevermore Bookshop – a woman by the name of Mina Wilde and her paramours Heathcliff Earnshaw, James Moriarty, and Allan Poe – intend to host a heathen wedding ceremony at Lachlan Hall where they will marry each other in a salacious mockery of sacred wedding vows!

Everyone in the village has received an invitation to this blasphemous ceremony. If you value the sanctity of your soul, we urge you not to attend this demonic wedding and instead join us at church for a prayer circle to pray for the souls of these sinners, so that they may see the error of their ways and repent from their unholy relationship, lest evil befall them and all who know them.

The prayer circle will be followed by a potluck tea.

CHAPTER 3

MINA

The minute Heathcliff, Quoth, and Morrie left for their appointment at Lachlan Hall, I slid out from behind my desk, picked up Oscar's lead, and slunk downstairs.

My mind reeled from that horrible email. Was Jen right? Was the reason why no one had RSVPed for my book launch because they didn't think anyone would actually read my book?

Was I *unrelatable?*

Was my writing career over before it had even begun?

I slumped on the sofa beneath the front window, which looked out onto Butcher Street and across the Nevermore Bookshop. Oscar dropped to the floor at my feet, ready in case I needed him for another task.

I could only make out the outline of the building, but I knew Nevermore so well that I could conjure the scene from my memories of the place – the lines of chairs set out in the Events room, the makeshift bar where Richard from the Rose & Wimple would serve book-themed drinks, the display stacked high with copies of my book (if I ever finished editing it), me wearing the outfit I'd specifically chosen for the occasion (black leather skirt, red bustier, red-and-black pinstripe jacket with sleeves rolled up and lapels covered in pins), and no one showed up.

It's not going to happen like that, Mina.

My friends and family would be there. Mrs. Ellis would make sure that the Spirit Seekers Society and her Naughty Knitting Circle would come. The guys wouldn't leave my side.

But I'd spent the last year turning Nevermore Bookshop into a successful business, ingratiating myself with writers and distributors and the publishing world. I thought that I'd been making friends and charming people, but when it came to the crunch, it was the same, dumb nonsense all over again.

People didn't want me because I was blind.

I wasn't good enough.

If I'd seen that email eighteen months ago, it would have broken my heart, in the same way that Marcus Ribald's rejection broke me. But I'd been toughened by everything I'd been through, and by all the negative criticism I received at the Meddleworth Writers Retreat.

Now, Jen's email made me sad for completely different reasons.

She was *wrong*.

If the publishing industry thought the same as her, then they were wrong, too.

I *existed*. People like me existed, too. We were everywhere. We might use a Braille display or screen reader to enjoy our fiction, but we still loved stories. And we deserved to be in those stories.

Part of the reason why I was so afraid when I first started losing my eyesight was because I didn't have any good stories about what it meant to be blind. All those hundreds of books I read growing up, the books that comforted me on my darkest days, not one of them had a blind heroine who got to be herself, fight crime, have adventures, or get the guys.

I wanted to give that story to people like me. That was why I was trying to make a big deal about the book launch, instead of just hiding away the way I tried to do after Marcus fired me. I thought that these people I'd worked with for months thought the same as me. I thought they *got* it.

But I was wrong.

My blood sizzled with rage at that. It made me feel as though they were all humouring the blind girl, pretending to encourage my writing until I needed them in my corner.

Fine. So none of my VIPs are coming to the book launch. I needed to figure out what I was going to do next. And staring at my woefully imperfect manuscript strewn across my office wasn't helping.

My boys weren't here, so the only thing that would fix this problem was a cup of tea.

I had Oscar drag my moping arse into the small kitchenette out the back of the studio. I put the kettle on to boil and set out my favorite cup – the one Quoth made me with a raised pattern of ravens sculpted around the rim.

I was just selecting a brew from the jars of loose leaf tea Quoth had thoughtfully labeled with Braille when I heard the door swing open behind me.

"I'm sorry, the studio is closed today," I called over my shoulder. Quoth was supposed to put a sign up out front, but sometimes he got so caught up in his artwork that he forgot—

"I know," a nervous voice said from the other side of the studio. Female, a local accent, and around my age, I thought. "I was actually looking for you. At least, I think I'm looking for you. You're Mina Wilde?"

"I sure am."

She phrased it like a question, so I felt as though I should answer.

The kettle whistled.

I tipped some loose leaf tea into a strainer and slotted my liquid level indicator over the edge of my cup, then poured in my hot water. The indicator beeped at me to tell me when I was a centimeter below the rim, and I stopped pouring.

"I hope you don't mind. I saw you through the window, and I know you're busy, but I had to try. My name is Maisie Collins. I heard that you're quite good at solving mysteries. I was wondering if you could help me." Her voice trembled with worry. "My friend James has gone missing."

"Missing?" I whirled around, wincing as hot tea splashed on my hand. "Have you told the police?"

"I did, but they didn't want to know about it."

"That doesn't sound like them." Inspector Hayes may lack imagination, but he did actually care about doing his job and keeping the community safe. I can't imagine him dismissing this worried girl. "I could talk to the inspector, perhaps. How long has James been missing?"

"Since yesterday evening. I'm going crazy with worry." Maisie grabbed the edge of the trestle table Quoth used for his art classes. She looked as though it was the only thing holding her upright. With her free hand, she dug around in her purse and held out something towards me. "I have some photographs on my phone."

"I'm sorry, I'm too blind to be able to see photographs. But you can describe him to me. Would you like a cup of tea?"

"Yes, please. Milk and two sugars. Do you need a hand?"

"Nope. I got this." I turned back to make another cup as Maisie continued. "So tell me about James."

"He's about twelve inches tall, with yellow feathers and an orange bill—"

"I'm sorry? He has *feathers?*"

"James is my pet duck. Did I not mention that?" Her voice warmed. "His full name is James Pond, Earl of Waddleton the Third. He's a purebred Peking drake. I'm worried that he might've been duck-napped."

As I brought Maisie's tea over to the table and sat down across from her, I found that with the large window facing Butcher Street behind her, I could make out her outline. She was at least a head taller than me, maybe almost as tall as Morrie, and she sat awkwardly in the chair, as though she was afraid of taking up space. She had a head of the most incredibly tight curls I'd ever seen. And she had a pet duck, which meant I liked her already.

"What makes you think that James has been duck-napped? Couldn't he simply have escaped? Why don't you tell me what happened from the beginning."

Maisie sipped her tea. When she spoke again, I could tell that she was trying not to cry. "James has a pen in my back garden where he sleeps and hangs out while I'm at work. Every night after work, I let him out and we go for a walk/paddle along the King's Copse stream, then we go inside and watch some Netflix together, and I put him to bed. But I came home from work yesterday and he was gone. There's a giant hole in the netting around his pen, but I don't think he could have done it himself. He's a very docile duck, and he's never escaped before. I've never even seen him try to chew on his pen. I'm so worried about him. I think my neighbor might have—"

"Might have what?"

Maisie swallowed hard. "My next-door neighbor, Stanley Clarke, has been complaining about James ever since I got him. I obeyed all the council laws when I put in James' pen. It's not illegal to keep a pet duck as long as he's contained and doesn't violate noise restrictions. James is a good duck! He hardly ever makes a peep, but Stanley keeps complaining to the council that he quacks all day long. The council came out to measure the noise volume and determined that James's quacks were within the acceptable decibel range. I think Stanley might have gotten sick of James and gone over when I wasn't home and… and…"

Maisie burst into tears.

My fingers toyed with the handle of my teacup. I shouldn't be entertaining this case. I was getting married in four days, and I had my book launch to salvage. My manuscript was still in tatters all over my office. And I had to figure out how to get the literati to pay attention to my book—

But maybe this is exactly what you need, a tiny voice in my head said. *A little detective work to remind you that you are wanted, that you have value. That you're relatable. Even if the book world doesn't want you, Argleton still needs you.*

Heathcliff, Morrie, and Quoth would tell me not to do this.

Well, they're not here, are they? But Maisie is. And she needs my help.

I reached across the table and offered my hand. "Maisie, you came to the right amateur bookshop detective. I'll take your case."

CHAPTER 4

QUOTH

"What are we going to do about this?" Heathcliff jabbed his finger at the note.

The three of us stood around the tattered remains of the chair covers. Cynthia had been called away on urgent tulle business, so with the door now firmly locked, I could transform into my human form.

I slumped onto one of Cynthia's designer sofas and piled handfuls of tattered fabric over my lower half. The words on that note burned inside my skull.

Someone wants to hurt Mina.

Morrie cracked his knuckles. "Simple. We find this note-writer and encourage them to take a long walk off an extremely short pier."

Heathcliff's black eyes blazed. "An excellent plan."

I swallowed. The two of them wouldn't hesitate to use violence if it meant protecting Mina. That was their way. They were, after all, two of literature's most notorious villains.

"Maybe we don't have to murder them?" I suggested lightly. "Maybe we simply convince them to stop trying to hurt Mina?"

"Right." Morrie made his fingers into little air quotes. "'Convince' them."

"Convince them with a rusty pitchfork," Heathcliff growled, as if Morrie's meaning wasn't obvious.

"Convince them by scooping their brains out of their skulls and using the empty vessel as a punch bowl."

Heathcliff's eyes lit up. "We do need a punch bowl for the wedding reception..."

Panic rose in my chest. "Yes, yes, I want to throttle this person as much as the two of you—"

"Good, then we're in agreement. Decapitation and brain scooping it is. I don't see why we're still standing around talking while there is a wedding saboteur out there with their head still attached to their body."

"—but maybe we could try a non-violent method of dissuading them first?" I suggested quietly. "Mina would not like knowing that we murdered someone before our wedding, even if that someone was trying to ruin it."

"*Non*-violent?" Morrie rubbed his chin. "Interesting."

Heathcliff picked up a handful of tattered chair covers and thrust it into my face. "Does it look like we're dealing with a nonviolent person?"

"Well, technically, all they've done is cut up some fabric and left a note. Maybe it was an accident."

The moment the words left my mouth, I knew they were wistful thinking. I just hated the idea that someone wanted to hurt Mina.

"This was no accident," Heathcliff growled. "Someone is trying to sabotage our wedding."

"And they're willing to use *any means necessary*." Morrie tapped his finger over the words.

I swallowed. *This isn't fair. Mina deserves the perfect wedding, not to be threatened with badly-glued notes.* "We should take this to the police."

"To Hayes and Wilson?" Heathcliff scoffed. "You think those fools are going to care about a few shredded chair covers and a note?"

"If we tell them, they'll advise us to cancel the wedding," Morrie said gravely. "I for one am not going to let this anonymous shit-stirrer keep me from making Mina Wilde my unlawfully wedded wife. I say we solve this ourselves."

"Non-violently?" I asked hopefully.

Heathcliff squeezed his fist. His dark eyes screwed shut as he struggled to gain control over his emotions. When he opened them again, his black eyes were hard as steel. "Fine. We try it your way. But only because you're right that Mina won't want to trip over a corpse on her way down the aisle. Which means that we don't tell her about this."

"We have to at least warn her of the danger," I said.

Heathcliff's eyes darted to the blood-red fabric of the ruined chair covers.

"I agree with Heathcliff," Morrie said. "I didn't get a chance to tell you, but she got an email from that editor Jen Whately this morning. Jen said that she wasn't interested in Mina's book because she didn't think a blind character was relatable. She thinks that Mina should rewrite the book without her heroine going blind."

No.

That's horrible.

Mina would be *crushed*.

Morrie closed his hand over my arm. "Don't fly off to her just yet, birdie."

"Mina must be so upset. You know how hard she's been trying to drum up press and literary interest in her book." That novel was Mina's soul laid bare. I knew how terrifying it was to put a piece of your soul on public display and have people not like it. "I have to be with her."

"*Exactly.* Mina's placed all her hopes on her novel doing well. And she's got our wedding, too. She shouldn't have to fear for her life on top of that."

"You *really* don't think we should tell her?"

Morrie and Heathcliff shook their heads.

"We'll find who's behind this and stop them, all nice and quiet and non-violent-like." Morrie cracked his knuckles. "I volunteer to take charge of this investigation. Think of it as my contribution to the wedding."

I didn't like keeping this a secret from Mina, but Morrie did have a point. I didn't want to do anything else to upset her. "Okay, where do we begin?"

"We start where we always begin," Morrie's eyes sparkle. "A list of enemies."

CHAPTER 5
MINA

After Maisie left, my phone read out the time. It was getting too late to start the hunt for James Pond today. The guys still weren't back yet. Usually, Morrie or Quoth cooked for us all, but I thought that after how hard they were working on the wedding, they might appreciate a night off from domestic chores.

I grabbed the key and Oscar's leash and set out in the direction of the village green.

A new Indian takeaway place had opened up across the green in the shop once occupied by the ill-fated Rasmussen Books. As I stepped through the door, I was greeted by a brief flashback to finding Mr. Rasmussen sprawled on the floor, murdered by a blow to the head from his own fake First Folio. But the delicious smell of spices and fresh naan bread shooed it away.

"Hello, Mina. Hello, Oscar," Chirag, the owner, called out to me. He pulled something from under the counter and handed it to me. "The whole family is looking forward to the wedding. We are even closing the shop for the night. I have a Braille menu for you."

"Thanks, Chirag." My fingers danced across the menu. So many good options. Morrie would have chicken jalfrezi, Quoth loved his tikka masala, and Heathcliff was all about beef vindaloo. And of course, we wanted naan bread and samosas. But did I want mango chicken or lamb balti—

The bell tinkled behind me. "Oh, hello, Mina." It was Denise, the post-lady. "I see we both couldn't be bothered cooking tonight. Where are your lovely almost-husbands?"

"They're up at Lachlan Hall, doing some last-minute wedding stuff."

"That's wonderful. We're all so looking forward to it. Your wedding will be the village event of the year. And how lovely to have those three men planning it all for you – you're a real modern lady." Denise patted my arm. "Bless his heart, but we never thought that Heathcliff would last in the village with that surly attitude of his. You've been so good for him. Now I can't imagine pub quiz night without him! And your Allan is quite the artist. I have one of his paintings on my wall. 'Kings Copse From the Air.' It's amazing the details he can paint with a bird's eye view. Does he use a drone?"

I couldn't help smiling. "Something like that."

"And your book launch is the very next day. You are a busy woman! All the members of the Spirit Seekers will be there, of course. We wouldn't miss seeing Argleton's favorite daughter publish her very own book."

From the couch in the corner, I heard someone snort. I figured that they must be watching something on their phone. Denise and I placed our orders and returned to talking about the book launch.

"Honestly, I'm a little nervous about it," I said, thinking about my empty email inbox and Jen's suggestion. "I poured my heart into this book, and I don't know if it will be as successful as I hope for. But I'm trying to stay positive."

"Heathcliff was telling me that you have a bunch of reviewers and fancy publisher types coming down from London. I can't believe it, our own little celebrity—"

"Yes, Mina has all the fancy, important friends, doesn't she?" a snarky voice snapped behind me.

I stiffened. I knew now that the person who snorted before wasn't on their phone. They were snorting at *me*.

I plastered a smile on my face, even though my heart was hammering a mile a minute. I didn't want to deal with this guy now, not when I was still raw from Jen's email.

"Hi, Wayne."

Wayne Bryant was a local poet. He'd been in Nevermore numerous times, trying to get us to stock his poetry books. Heathcliff warned me that if I humored Wayne, I'd live to regret it. No matter how many times I explained that our customers didn't really buy poetry, Wayne refused to give up. Eventually, I took pity on him and let him put three of his books on the poetry shelf. I thought that would get him to leave us alone for a bit.

Reader, I was wrong again.

Wayne started coming in every day to move his books from the dusty poetry shelf to our front display. He shoved them under customer's noses, harassing them until they brought copies out of pity. He wanted to do a poetry reading. I explained that he needed to pay for the use of the Events room and I wouldn't be calling in my literary contacts to listen to him read his meandering villanelles about the various farm animals he encounters. (Wayne's the local large animal vet.) Wayne threw a bunch of books on the floor and stomped on them on his way out.

One day I returned from my lunch break to discover Wayne tearing down the posters advertising my book launch and yelling about nepotism and favoritism. We banned him from the shop. Heathcliff got to utter his four favorite words: "I told you so," and Wayne has hated me ever since.

"You should bow down, Denise, and kiss her feet, worship her creative brilliance," Wayne spat out. "That's what Mina really wants. She's going to make a name for herself with her bookshop and her industry contacts and her fancy friends, and bugger the rest of us."

The cruel tone in his voice made me want to run away, but I stood my ground. Wayne might not have a problem confronting me, but he was terrified of Heathcliff. *He's only saying this to my face because I'm alone.*

"Honey, don't be like that." Wayne's wife, Nora, tried to drag him back to his seat. Nora was the loveliest woman. She was a member of Mrs. Ellis' Naughty Knitting Club and regularly came into the bookshop to buy racy romance novels. "Mina's done so much to support the village. Did you know she donated all the picture books for the library summer read-a-thon?"

"Of course she did. Because Mina loves everyone fawning over her. She only supports the writers that she likes. But when it comes to poetry that tells the truth about the world, she can't be bothered to make an effort. Where's my fancy book launch? Where are all the reviewers and London literary agents for me?"

"I'm sorry that we couldn't sell your poetry book, Wayne," I said brightly, trying to allay the tension. "Sometimes there's just no accounting for the public's taste, right? I mean, look at Dan Brown..."

"It's got nothing to do with taste. You and that bastard Heathcliff deliberately sabotaged my book sales. You stuck my collection on the bottom shelf in a forgotten corner while signs about your upcoming book are in all the windows. And when I tried to tell the truth about your elitism, you kicked me out of the shop."

"You got kicked out because you—"

"You think that no one sees through this veneer of nice you wear, Mina. But you're just like your mother. You only want one thing – fame and fortune and riches. And you don't care who you stomp on to get it."

"Wayne, stop this right now!" Nora grabbed their order off the counter and shoved her husband towards the door. "I'm sorry about him, Mina. Wayne's having a bad day. Bad week, actually. He goes up hunting deer on the Lachlan estate, but he hasn't caught a thing! It's just rotten luck, but then he gets wound up and doesn't mean it—"

"I mean every word!" Wayne yelled over his shoulder. "Mina Wilde is rotten, and I'm not going to stand for it anymore. I'll make sure that no one reads a single word you write!"

CHAPTER 6
MORRIE

"Obviously, whoever is behind this intends to sabotage our wedding." I perused the drawers of the Georgian sideboard until I located a pad of paper and a Montblanc pen. I tapped my long fingers against the paper. "Who in the village doesn't want Mina to get married?"

We all looked at each other and said at the same time, "Dorothy Ingram."

"She's been railing against our 'unholy union' for weeks," Heathcliff growled. "When I tried to book the community hall for the reception, she complained to the council. That's why we had to move here."

"She put up those horrible posters about her prayer meeting all over the village." Quoth shuddered. "Maybe she decided she'd have to do more than pray us away."

I wrote Dorothy's name on the top of my pad and underlined it three times. "She seems the most likely suspect, but if we've learned anything from Mina's previous investigations, it's that we need to be thorough. Can we think of anyone else who might want to destroy Mina's happiness?"

"There's that writer, Wayne Bryant," Quoth said. "He's been into the shop a couple of times trying to get us to stock his dreary poetry collection."

Heathcliff made a face. "The one with the poems that are worse than the Poet Prince Edward's oeuvre?"

Oof, Wayne's poetry must be *terrible*.

"That's the one." Quoth fidgeted with a tattered strand of gold ribbon, his fire-rimmed eyes dark with worry. "I heard him complaining at the pub the other week that Nevermore Bookshop was guilty of literary nepotism and Mina is using her clout as the bookshop owner to turn her book into a bestseller. He might be bitter enough to want to hurt Mina."

"Doesn't the man know that no one wants to read poetry," Heathcliff snapped. "Not even *good* poetry."

"'Poetry lifts the veil from the hidden beauty of the world, and makes familiar objects be as if they were not familiar'," Quoth quoted, his long eyelashes tangling together. "Percy Bysshe Shelley."

"Poetry is a load of rubbish words strung together by weepy beatniks who believe the weather has feelings," Heathcliff tapped his chin proudly. "Heathcliff."

I wrote Wayne's name underneath Dorothy. "Anyone else?"

"What about someone Mina put behind bars?" Quoth asked. "She's ruined quite a few nefarious schemes with her clever sleuthing."

The problem with being engaged to a woman who solved mysteries in a quaint English village was that she made a lot of enemies. However, because Mina was actually quite good at her hobby, she'd managed to put quite a few of them behind bars, where they couldn't get her. Unless...

"It could be a hit job," Heathcliff said. "I wouldn't put it past Angus Donahue."

"Angus Donahue is an ex-cop. If he did this, it wouldn't be

nearly so messy. If this is a hit, then it's a bloody terrible one." I held up a handful of torn fabric. "I don't think this is the work of a hardened criminal. It's too petty. But I'll check with my contacts in the underground, in case one of the criminals Mina put behind bars is out and looking for revenge. You two leave this to me, I promise that I'll take care of our little problem."

"That's what I'm afraid of," Quoth murmured.

"I made you a promise, birdie," I grinned as I hid my crossed fingers behind my back. "Absolutely no violence."

CHAPTER 7

MINA

"How goes the wedding preparations?" I asked as I greeted the guys at the door to the flat with my arms full of takeaway containers. My mood had been flip-flopping wildly since I got back from Chirag's – between Jen's email and Maisie's case and that awful confrontation with Wayne, I was a bit of a mess. But hearing my guys clomping up the stairs to our flat cheered me up. "Have Cynthia and Iwan got every event professional in the Loamshire County hunkered down in their war room?"

"Er, yes, everything's fine." Heathcliff breezed past me. He collected four kittens off his chair before collapsing into it. The kittens commenced climbing over him as if he were their own personal jungle gym, which I suppose he was. "The wedding is going perfectly. Absolutely no saboteurs trying to ruin it."

"What?"

I heard a cork slide from the neck of a whisky bottle Heathcliff pulled from some dark recess of his coat. "Nothing. Don't worry about it. The chair covers arrived. They look nice."

As Morrie sauntered into the room, Quoth perched on his

shoulder, he brushed his lips over my ear. "Nothing Surly O'Hara over there won't fix, Mina."

"That's good to hear," I grinned. "Because let's just say that the book launch isn't going quite how I planned, and I had a run-in with our friend Wayne today. I need *something* in my life to go without a hitch."

"What about Wayne?" Heathcliff jerked forward, nearly tossing Peanut across the room. Luckily, Morrie picked the kitten out of the air before she became another victim of Heathcliff's rage. "What did that bastard do now?"

"Nothing really. He cornered me at the takeaways and yelled about how I'm basically the Brutus of the book world because I wouldn't set up a free launch for his poetry collection. He made a threat about making sure the launch was a flop, but he was blowing off steam. It's nothing to worry about." I swallowed. "I hope."

"I'll be the judge of that." Heathcliff cracked his knuckles menacingly.

"Honestly, he probably doesn't even have to do anything to sabotage my launch. I seem to be doing a fine job of that on my own." I drop Oscar's harness one-handed onto the hook. He was officially off-duty. He tapped my knee, excited for his dinner. Chirag had made him a special 'dog curry' of rice, carrots, and potatoes.

"Morrie told us about the letter." Quoth unlooped the bags from my arm and led me to my seat opposite Heathcliff by the fire. "I know how hard you've worked, but you can't let one setback stop you from telling your story—"

Morrie rummaged around in the kitchen, and I jumped as a cork popped against the ceiling.

"It's fine," I muttered, slumping down in the seat. "It doesn't matter. I don't even care about Jen or what she thinks."

"Mina—"

"You finished editing your book yet?" Heathcliff asked as he grabbed his vindaloo. "Not that it needed any further work. It was perfect."

"You're just saying that because you're the one who edited it."

"And I did a damn fine job. Typos are afraid of me."

"I believe that." I changed the subject so I didn't have to answer any more probing questions about the book. "Do you guys know a girl named Maisie Collins?"

"Doesn't she write for the Argleton Gazette?" Morrie said from the kitchen. "She covers the town council meetings and writes thrilling exposés about the pig that got loose in the farmer's market."

"Maisie came to visit me today. Someone took her pet duck, James Pond."

At the mention of 'duck,' Grimalkin's head popped up between my legs, ears standing tall with interest. I patted her head. "No, Grandma, this isn't a duck for you to eat. But I think there might be a bit of haddock in that bag for you."

"James Pond is a brilliant name." Morrie handed me a glass of wine. "I like this woman already. I assume you took the case."

"Of course she didn't." Heathcliff eased himself into the chair opposite me. He put his feet up on the footrest between us, his toe stroking the edge of my foot. "Mina's got enough to do between re-editing her perfectly edited book and getting ready for the wedding."

"Actually..." I grinned.

"Mina."

"I can't help who I am! Besides, if you saw Maisie crying over James, you wouldn't have been able to say no, either."

"Want to bet?" Heathcliff muttered.

"Could I help, gorgeous?" Morrie angled the lamp behind my chair so that it lit up the space in front of me, and he placed a plate of half mango chicken and half lamb balti on my lap. Heathcliff's favorite kitten, Maximilian, tried to steal a piece of lamb from the side of the plate, but I plopped him down on the floor.

"Morrie doesn't have time to help. He has his own wedding-related job to do, doesn't he?" Heathcliff tossed a piece of meat to Max.

"Hey, that was mine!" Morrie cried.

"Well, I can hardly give him vindaloo, can I? It would hurt his little stomach."

"What wedding-related job?" I asked.

"It's not important," Quoth said hurriedly. "Except that Morrie needs to do it quickly and neatly and *non-violently.*"

"I am an expert multi-tasker," Morrie purred. "Why, just the other night I had my tongue buried inside Mina while I stroked Heathcliff's—"

"Pass the garlic naan!" Heathcliff boomed.

"If you want to help, I'd love that. I need you to check around about Maisie's neighbor, Stanley Clarke. He's been complaining to the council about James Pond, so he seems a likely suspect in this duck-napping. Quoth, I thought maybe you talk to some of the other local birds, see if anyone has seen any fowl play." I patted Oscar, who lay across my feet and used his nose to nudge away kittens who tried to come for his dinner. "Oscar and I are going over to Maisie's house in the morning to take a look at the crime scene."

Heathcliff perked up. "If you find this duck, does it mean Morrie will cook us his delicious duck à l'orange for dinner?"

"No. James is a purebred duck who is Maisie's best friend. We are not eating him."

"Fine." Heathcliff tossed another piece of Morrie's chicken to Maximilian. "Then pass the rice. And remember, this duck may have your attention now, but in four days, we are marrying you, and neither man nor feathered beast will tear us asunder."

TEXT MESSAGE HISTORY BETWEEN JAMES MORIARTY AND DOROTHY INGRAM

Dorothy Ingram, as I live and breathe, how's life as a repressed do-gooder?

Who is this? How did you get this number?

This is James Moriarty, from Nevermore Bookshop. All you need to know is that I have my methods.

I thought it was time we had a chat about the chair covers.

I don't know what you're talking about.

You've been very naughty, haven't you? Usually, I like naughty women, but in this case, you're attempting to ruin my wedding. I suggest you stop immediately.

Stop the prayer circle? Never. You cannot silence the word of God.

You ripped up the chair covers and left Mina a threatening note.

No.

Not me.

I couldn't have done that. I've been in Grimdale looking after my sister Megan. She had a nasty fall. Ask anyone in the village. They'll be able to tell you. I've been there practically 24/7.

A likely story.

Contact me again and I'll report you to the police.

Will you? Would you like everyone to know all about your dirty little secret?

I don't know what you're talking about.

Yes, you do. Come on, Dorothy. You're a religious nutter, but you're not stupid. Remember a little visit you made to a certain hospital, for a certain procedure…

You don't know anything.

Play coy if you like. You can have your little prayer circle and pray for our lost, corrupted souls. But stay away from our wedding and no one has to know your secret.

CHAPTER 8

MINA

The next morning, Morrie woke me in bed with a cup of tea and a cinnamon roll from Oliver's bakery.

"Where are Heathcliff and Quoth?" I patted the empty bed beside me. I was used to waking up with Heathcliff's arm draped over me and Quoth curled into my shoulder.

"They're off on important wedding business," Morrie said as he clinked his teacup against mine. "I have you all to myself. Whatever shall we do with our morning?"

His lips brushed my neck, sending a shiver of delight down my spine. It would be so easy to lie back in our soft bed and let Morrie do all sorts of filthy things to me.

But that wouldn't help Maisie find James Pond. I gave Morrie a light shove.

"We've got work of our own to do today. I'm going to Maisie's house to look at the crime scene and maybe try to talk to her neighbor. Are you going to come?"

"I never say no to snooping. But I need to stop by Argleton Presbyterian on the way."

"Morrie," I frowned. "Don't tell me you're going after Dorothy Ingram. She's harmless, and remember, we know her dirty little secret from when we were investigating the Banned Book Club murders. She got pregnant out of wedlock and got an abortion. She talks a big game because she likes to look good in front of her church friends, but she can't do anything to mess up our wedding or the whole village will know about her secret abortion. So let her have her little prayer meeting."

"I know that, and you know that, but I think that Dorothy needs a reminder." Morrie held up his hands in mock surrender. "A *non-violent* reminder, I promise. Come on, gorgeous, let's get going."

I finished my tea, rolled out of bed, and headed over to the portable rack I used as a closet. I chose a pair of red cuffed trousers with little black cats leaping all over them. I couldn't actually see the cats, but Quoth went shopping with me and described them, and they sounded like my kind of trousers.

One of the things I worried about when I lost my sight was that I wouldn't get any joy from fashion any longer, but it's simply not true. If anything, I appreciate fashion on a new level now. Because I couldn't get so distracted by colors and patterns, I shopped based on *texture*. It was fun to have people describe patterns and colors to me, and I would always remember a garment by the way someone described it.

Like my wedding dress.

I reached into the back of the closet and stroked the garment bag. I designed it myself and Mrs. Ellis and her knitting club created it for me, since sewing was a bit difficult for me now. It was a lovely ivory silk with a tight corset bodice, and layers of tulle to create this incredible layered skirt. I didn't think I wanted a white dress, but Mum insisted, and I felt like Stephanie Seymour when I wore it.

I pulled back my hand. Today wasn't about me. Thankfully, Heathcliff had all of the wedding arrangements under control. And I wasn't thinking about my book. Not at all.

Today, I was going to solve Maisie's case and prove that I still had worth.

On with a red shirt with puffed sleeves, my leather jacket, and my trusty scuffed old Docs, a matching red bandana for Oscar, and we were ready to leave. Morrie, however, wasn't. We had to wait another ten minutes while he shaved and got his hair looking just the way he liked it. I had to admit, though, that when he exited the bathroom and slid his arm through mine, he smelled amazing.

We walked together up Butcher Street and across the village green to Argleton Presbyterian Church. Oscar and I waited beside the lychgate while Morrie strode towards the church. I might believe that Dorothy Ingram was basically harmless, but that didn't mean I wanted to talk to her. She'd made it clear numerous times that she disapproved of me and my relationship and everything I stood for. I wouldn't give her the satisfaction of letting her know that her efforts to derail our wedding mattered to me.

Morrie returned a few minutes later, a note of triumph in his voice. "Good news, gorgeous. She wasn't there, but the notice for her prayer meeting is gone, and Father Clarence tells me that she decided not to do it. I guess she did listen to reason after all."

"Listen to reason? Morrie, you didn't tell me that you've already been talking to her."

"I did nothing illegal. I merely reminded her of the little secret of hers that we know." Morrie practically skipped down the road. "She won't be bothering us again."

We turned down a narrow cobblestoned street that curved behind the church, crossed a footbridge over the stream, and headed along the footpath in front of a row of neat brick townhouses.

Maisie lived in a block of smaller one- and two-bedroom

townhouses on tiny sections. She flung open the door before we even knocked. "Hi, Mina, hi, Oscar. I'm so glad you came. I kept thinking that James would appear in the middle of the night, huddled up on top of the blankets the way he likes, but he's still missing."

"We're going to get to the bottom of this, Maisie. We're not about to let a duck-napping go uninvestigated." I gestured to Morrie. "This is Morrie, one of my fiancés. He's going to help me with the investigation."

Maisie sounded worried. "Do you have any experience?"

"Oh, yes. I have an uncanny knack for seeing deep inside the mind of the criminally inclined," Morrie said with that cheeky tone in his voice. I didn't have to see him to know that he was winking at me.

Maisie led us out to the back yard and showed us James Pond's pen. I don't know what I was imagining when she described it to me, but I certainly didn't expect the duck palace she created. Morrie described to me how James had a large children's paddling pool, a bunch of plants for him to hide in, three decks at different levels for him to sun himself on, a palatial mansion for when he needed private time indoors, and a bunch of food stations and toys.

Maisie crouched down behind the duck mansion. "Here's the hole."

I ran my fingers along the edges of the wire netting. It was rough to the touch, the wires warped. "It's quite a small hole, only just large enough for a duck. I'm surprised someone was able to reach both hands in here and drag him out."

"James is a friendly duck. If you stuck your arm through, he'd come right up and headbutt your hand, and it would be easy to grab him." Maisie's voice rose. "I can't believe someone would do this."

"Mina, there's a footprint here," Morrie said. I heard his phone camera click.

I ran over. Morrie took my hand and directed me to feel the earth near the fence. My fingers brushed over damp earth, feeling the lines of a well-formed shoeprint. I didn't know enough about shoes, but it had distinctive herringbone stripes across the print. I thought it would be pretty easy to match...if we found the duck-napper.

"This fence connects to the neighbor you told me about?" I asked Maisie.

"Yes. Stanley lives there. He's the one who reported me to the council because of James Pond's quacking. He claimed that he loved birds but that James wasn't the right sort of bird for this area. And now James is gone and—"

"Good riddance."

I stood up and turned toward the voice. Oscar growled low in his throat.

I could make out the shape of a man's head peeking over the fence. He sounded older, maybe around Mrs. Ellis' age, and grumpy enough to give Heathcliff a run for his money.

"That bird was a menace," Stanley snarled. "It quacked all day and all night, and when she walked it around the neighborhood, it pooped all over the sidewalk."

"I picked up all of James Pond's poop," Maisie snapped back. "And the council said it wasn't against the rules to keep James."

"The duck needed stimulation during the day. You shouldn't leave an animal like that alone for so long. Ducks are social animals."

"I have to *work*, Stanley. We can't all afford to sit on our asses at home all day, spying on our neighbors."

"I'm not spying! I never spy!"

"You do, too. I've seen you on your back porch with those

binoculars of yours. And Darcy McKlenn from three doors down said that someone reported her art shed for violating planning laws. That was you, wasn't it?"

"That construction is two feet too close to the boundary line!"

"It's an art shed! It's not hurting anyone!" Maisie sounded close to tears. "You're allowed to be a miserable old man on your own property, but how could you take James? Where is he? Is he okay? If you've hurt him, I'll…I'll…I'll sic Morrie on you!"

"I'd never hurt an innocent bird when it's the owner's fault it misbehaves." Stanley snapped. "I hope that you've learned your lesson about keeping a drake."

He stomped away. A moment later, his porch door slammed shut, followed by a beautiful singsong noise that must have been his radio or something.

"He certainly made it seem as though he was guilty," Morrie said. "I think we need a little investigation."

CHAPTER 9
MINA

orrie, Oscar, and I walked back to Nevermore Bookshop. Morrie tapped away on his phone. "The pattern on that boot was rather distinctive. I'm hunting for a match. So far, I can confirm that our duck-napper was definitely not wearing a pair of this season's Versace loafers."

"That's useful, thank you. Did you go directly to the Versace website because you're looking for a match, or because you want new shoes?"

"Your lack of faith in my sleuthing skills astounds me." Morrie went to insert the key into the door of the shop. "Odd. The door is unlocked."

"Heathcliff and Quoth must be back from Lachlan Hall."

Morrie shoved the door all the way. "Heathcliff wouldn't leave the front door open. Customers might come in."

"True. Maybe it's—Argh!"

A shadow reached out and grabbed me, yanking me inside.

"There you are, darling! I've been trying to find you everywhere."

I squinted into the gloomy hallway. None of my lamps were

turned on, which meant I could barely even see her outline. I gripped Oscar's harness. "Mum, what are you doing here?"

"I needed to speak to Heathcliff about the wedding, but he's not here, so I suppose you'll do. I'm having some problems with the favors. My monogramming machine doesn't like doing four initials."

Inwardly, I groaned. When Mum offered to craft our wedding favors as her gift to us, I thought that sounded like a nice, *safe* way to involve her in the wedding plans without having our special day hijacked by her latest scheme. I should have known better. It turned out that Mum had purchased an industrial embroidery machine that she could program to do all kinds of designs, and she was trying to set herself up as a personalised monogramming business.

Of all her business ideas, monogramming was at least one of the most legitimate. She made actual handkerchiefs and towels instead of the NFTs of Grimalkin that she was trying to sell before. But I knew it was only a matter of time before 'Helen's Monograms' became susceptible to Mum's...Mumness.

"That machine takes up your entire living room," I pointed out. "Surely it can manage to embroider four initials instead of two."

"I'm sure it can, too, but the instructions are all in German. Andy's taking a class online, but he's not proficient enough to decipher the manual. He can, however, tell me that my hamster smells. *Dein hamster riecht.* Isn't he clever?"

Behind me, the door swung open, and I caught a whiff of Heathcliff's wild, peaty scent and the fresh lightness of Quoth's presence. Quoth's arm slid around my waist, pulling me against him. He knew I often needed a steady presence when dealing with my mother.

I prepared myself for battle. "Mum, you don't have a hamster."

"I know *that*, but you never know when it might come in handy. Anyway, since I can't get all of your initials onto the cloth napkins, I thought, maybe we'd just put an M on them."

Morrie perked up. "M for Morrie? I approve."

"M for *Mina*," Mum corrected. "And maybe an H for Helen, since I *did* go to all the trouble of making the favors. It would be a huge boost to my business to get in front of all those people."

"You want the wedding favors at our wedding to be monogrammed with M&H? Morrie and Heathcliff?" Morrie asked lightly. "People will just think we forgot to add the other two."

"You're right, that is a little confusing. What about just an H? H for Helen. Since it *is* my machine we're using." Mum beamed. "That's perfect. There will be so many people there who might want their own monogrammed items. It would be good for them to know who I was. Maybe I can add a little business card, too..."

"What about if you did a little picture instead?" Quoth suggested. He grabbed a sketch pad from his satchel and started drawing. "Like this?"

"I really do think that the letter H is our best bet...oh." Mum peered over Quoth's shoulder. "That's really quite good. Maybe you and I could work something out. I don't suppose you happen to read German?"

"What is it?" I tapped the corner of the sketch. Quoth would usually explain what he was drawing to me as he worked.

"It's a surprise," Quoth kissed me lightly on the cheek.

I threw up my hands. "Argh. You lot! This surprise wedding thing is going to your heads. Fine, stay down here and plot things. I'm going upstairs to make a duck-napping board."

CHAPTER 10

QUOTH

That evening, I sat across from Mina while she added string to her duck-napping board, connecting Stanley Clarke with a timeline of events in James Pond's disappearance. A list of questions had been taped in Braille next to him, including 'Council report? Footprint? A tool used to cut wires?'

"I called Pleasure to Meat You today," she murmured as she worked. "I wanted to see if anyone had come in with a dead Peking duck to butcher, but Harris said the only birds he'd seen recently were Mrs. Ellis and her friends. Apparently, they all think our local butcher is quite handsome. So this means that if the duck-napper killed James Pond, they buried the evidence..."

"I have to ask this, artist to artist," I said. "Should you really be throwing yourself into a case so close to the wedding and the—"

"I wonder if we could sneak Oscar into Stanley's garden to sniff around..." Mina tapped her phone screen.

"—book launch? Are you *sure* that you're not trying to distract yourself because you are nervous?"

"I'm not nervous." She glared at me. "I'm *not*."

"Mina."

"So what if not a single person from the book industry cares about my novel? So what if I really am unrelatable? So what if there's a distinct possibility we ordered all those scones from Oliver and no one shows up to eat them? At this rate, I think that I might cancel it, maybe do it a bit later in the year when I'm more prepared, after I've done some more editing."

"No, Mina, you're not thinking of editing the book like Jen said? It won't be the story you want to tell."

"What does it matter if it's my story when no one will read it?" Mina chewed on a strand of her hair. "Besides, I'm too busy with the James Pond case to worry about it now. Do you think you could head out tonight and ask some of the local birds—"

"Quoth, can we have a minute?" Heathcliff called from the stairwell.

"I'm just about to go help Mina look for the duck—"

"This is *important*."

There was no point explaining to Heathcliff that the duck was important to Mina. I followed him and Morrie downstairs. Heathcliff unlocked the shop door and led the two of us out into the street.

"I figured she won't hear us out here," he whispered. "We need a debrief. Quoth and I spent most of the day putting out fires up at Lachlan Hall. We didn't get to do any investigating about the note, but I have finally found a place that will rent us enough chair covers. They could only do pink ribbons, so Iwan is at his house now, sewing us enough gold ribbons for the ceremony. That man is a lifesaver."

"Why don't you marry him?" Morrie sniped.

"Trust me, I considered it," Heathcliff shot back. "Morrie, do you have an update for us about Wayne Bryant and Dorothy Ingram?"

"I do," Morrie rubbed his palms together. "I haven't got to Wayne yet, but I've taken care of Dorothy."

Unease stabbed at my chest. What *exactly* did Morrie mean by that? "You didn't—"

"Relax, birdie. All I did was remind her about the dirt we have on her, that if she doesn't want her little secret splashed across the front page of the Argleton Gazette, she needs to leave the wedding alone. She denied everything, but she canceled her prayer meeting and Father Clarence said that she left the village to visit her sister in Grimdale. Problem solved. The wedding can go ahead, and we don't have to worry about any more rotten little notes—"

"Heathcliff, there you are! I need to talk to you."

We turned toward the voice. Oliver ran from the bakery, his face coated in flour, his features grim.

All my soul within me burned with unease.

"It's about the wedding cake," Oliver began. "Something's happened."

Heathcliff went very still, his hands balled into fists at his sides. He turned slowly, and I sensed that Oliver was in grave danger. "What kind of something?"

"I've been working on it all week. A five-tier cake made to look like a stacked bookshelf, with all of Mina's favorite books, and a black raven on top. Do you have any idea how difficult it is to sculpt a black raven out of icing? Anyway, I did it, and it was amazing, but—"

"*Was* amazing?" Heathcliff said, his voice eerily calm.

I swallowed down my dread.

"I can't explain it..." Ollie screwed up his face. He stepped backwards, holding the door to the bakery kitchen open so we could see inside.

I peered around Heathcliff's shoulder and gasped.

Every surface of Ollie's usually pristine kitchen was covered in cake. There was cake smeared on the ceiling and dribbling down the walls, cake wiped across the floor in giant swoops, and cake dripping from the light fixtures and extractor vents like delicious stalactites.

"I don't understand how this could have happened," Ollie stammered. "I stepped out to help the delivery man with my flour order. I left this door open for a *moment*, and when I came back inside, I found this horror show. It must've been a huge gust of wind to topple a heavy cake like that and smear it everywhere. Maybe it wasn't even the wind. I mean, there's that escaped patient from Crixley wandering around…"

I looked at Heathcliff. We were both thinking the same thing.

This is no accident.

Heathcliff glared at Morrie. "What did you say about Dorothy Ingram not being a problem anymore?"

"I'm so sorry," Ollie rubbed his eyes. "I've been working my ass off on that cake. I think it was the greatest thing I'd ever made. And on top of all the trouble we've been having with the new delivery service. The ordering app is janky and someone keeps stealing our deliveries off people's doorsteps before they can get them—"

"Oliver, we don't care."

"Right, yes, not your problem. Again, I'm so sorry guys, but your wedding is the day after tomorrow, and I have to go down to London for my sister's baby shower. I don't have time to start again. I can put you in touch with a couple of local cake designers, and you can see if they're available, but it's a busy time of year so you may not be able to get something as elaborate."

Morrie patted Ollie's shoulder. "I offer you my forgiveness… and a piece of advice."

"What's that?"

Morrie glanced over at Heathcliff, then back to Oliver. "Run."

Oliver opened his mouth like he might apologize again, then thought better of it and broke off into a run, disappearing across the town green.

I stared down at the carnage of what had once been a triumph of the art of icing. A long, mournful 'croooak' escaped my throat.

"What do you propose we do now?" Morrie said.

"We do what's in our nature," Heathcliff growled. "We get *villainous.*"

CHAPTER II
HEATHCLIFF

Quoth went quickly upstairs to make sure that Mina was safely tucked up in bed. He returned in human form, wearing black from head to toe, his waterfall of dark hair tied back off his neck and a grave expression on his face.

He did not ask us to be non-violent.

Good. Because I was in the mood to cause a little carnage.

People in this town had detested me ever since I arrived here, and I could deal with that because I had my books and my whisky and my foul, dark thoughts. I've read my own book – I knew the monster that I'd become. If I hid myself away from people and refused to let anyone in, I couldn't do the kind of damage that had destroyed the soul of Wuthering Heights after my last heartbreak.

But then Mina came along, and suddenly, I didn't want to be a monster anymore, unless I was *her* monster. She made me want to be better, to *believe* that I could actually have a home here with her and Morrie and Quoth, a home that I wouldn't tear apart with my own cruelty.

She made me laugh, a feat long believed impossible. She made me feel like I had sunshine in my veins.

That was why I wanted to give her this big, perfect wedding. Mina deserved the whole world. The thought of someone like Dorothy or Wayne trying to dull Mina's light after everything that Mina had gone through to get to this point made me see red.

I saw red now – big splotches in my vision that coalesced into a film of blood. My hands balled into fists. The whole world narrowed to a bloody, stabby point where I took the saboteur's neck in my fingers and squeezed and squeezed...

Morrie grabbed me by the shoulders. "You've never looked more attractive to me than with that murderous gleam in your eyes, but we need to think about this intellectually, the way Mina would. Our saboteur would have only just left the scene of the crime. They couldn't have gone down Butcher Street or we would have seen them when we stepped outside, so they must have headed up towards the green. The pub is full of people. Let's go and see if anyone saw anything."

It took a few moments for Morrie's words to sink through the red haze of my rage. I nodded and allowed him to drag me up towards the pub.

Immediately, we saw a useful source of information. Mrs. Ellis and her friends from the Spirit Seekers Society sat at a table near the entrance. They'd have eyes on anyone walking across the village green. Morrie dragged us around a couple of loud birds splashing in the fountain and straight to their table.

"Good evening, ladies," Morrie leaned in close, working his charm. "We're looking for the perpetrator of a terrible crime in Oliver's bakery. The fiend would have come this way. Did you see anything?"

"We saw that Hughes boy peeing on the gate of the grave-yard," Sylvia Blume chortled.

"And Wanda Lannahan having a huge barney with her husband beside the fountain," Gloria added with a grin.

"And one of Cynthia's wait staff is lurking in the corner, wearing a baseball cap *inside*," Penny slapped the table with glee. "She'll be beside herself with embarrassment when I tell her."

Mrs. Ellis ignored Morrie and pulled *me* down so I was practically sitting on her lap. "I didn't see where he came from, but Wayne Bryant headed across the green in the direction of the church. *And* he was being all furtive, leaping between the shrubberies, trying not to be seen."

"Was he just?"

"What about Dorothy Ingram?" Morrie's icicle eyes glinted with malice. "Has she been out tonight?"

"Oh yes, old busybody herself was here earlier. She scolded me for drinking on the eve of the Sabbath." Mrs. Ellis raised her wine glass happily. "I told her if it was good enough for the Son of God, it was good enough for me. She slunk away after that, probably headed to her sister's. She's been looking after her poorly sister in Grimdale, and seems to be there every spare moment these days. Just as well, so the rest of us can get on with our sinning in peace."

We left the ladies and hightailed it across the green to the churchyard. When we stepped through the lychgate, all was in darkness. I tried the doors to the church and the bell tower, but they were locked up tight. Morrie clicked on the flashlight on his phone, and we wandered between the graves, searching for Wayne.

Morrie shone the light into the windows of the groundskeeper's shed, then pulled back, shaking his head.

"I think Old Mac must be sneaking in here for an afternoon snooze instead of tending the graves," Morrie said. "There's an entire *pile* of blankets in the corner. And look at this."

He swept the flashlight over the ground near where a dripping hose had been coiled up. Perfectly preserved in the dirt was the impression of a shoe.

"This is interesting." Morrie rubbed his chin. "See those herringbone stripes? This bootprint is the same as the one we found in Maisie's back garden, at the sight of the infamous duck-napping."

"I'm not thinking about a missing duck right now," I growled.

"Fine, fine. I don't think Wayne is still hiding here. We'll catch up with him later. I don't know where he lives. Let's try Dorothy first. She's down past the town hall."

As we hurried across the street in the direction of Dorothy Ingram's house, Morrie pointed out the row of townhouses behind the church, where the duck had gone missing. We doubled back around the edge of the village to get to Dorothy's house. She wasn't there, either, her windows dark. But her car was in the driveway.

"Maybe she really did go to her sister's house..." Morrie murmured. "But why didn't she take her car?"

"Let's find out," I growled. "Call an Uber. Find an address."

Morrie tapped away on his phone. A few minutes later, a sleek black car pulled up and we climbed in. The town of Grimdale was a fifteen-minute drive, which gave me plenty of time to imagine all the ways I might convince this woman to leave Mina and our wedding alone.

When we pulled up at the cottage of Dorothy's sister, a sliver of doubt crept in. Quoth's worried voice echoed in my head.

Mina would not like knowing that we murdered someone before our wedding, even if that someone was trying to ruin it.

I loved our woman, but she was in possession of a set of pesky *morals*.

The bird was right. If Mina found out we'd hurt an old lady – even that vengeful witch, Dorothy Ingram – she'd be upset. She'd always believed that I was better than the man in my books turned out to be.

As tempting as it was to go full Heathcliff, I had to be better for her.

I grabbed Morrie's hand as he swung out of the car. "We're doing this non-violently," I hissed.

He made a face. "You're no fun."

We strode up the path and rang the bell. An elderly woman with rosy cheeks and a frilly pink nightcap answered the door. "Hello? Are you lovely young gentlemen from the council? I've been calling and calling about the water meter—"

Morrie shrugged. "Sure. We're from the council. Megan Ingram? We need to speak to Dorothy."

The woman's face instantly transformed into a frown. "I'm afraid she's not here."

"She's not with you?" Morrie raised one of his perfect eyebrows. "We were led to believe that she's been helping you after you had a fall."

"I think you've been led up the garden path." The woman tapped her legs. "As you can see, I'm fine and dandy. And Dorothy wouldn't help me out of a hole in the ground. We don't exactly get along. If you're looking for my do-gooder sister, she's probably at that church of hers, praying for the salvation of my heathen soul. Pot brownie?"

She held out a tray filled with delicious-smelling chocolate brownies. I declined, but Morrie took one and bit down happily. "These are delicious. Thank you. We shall leave you to your evening."

"Wait, didn't you want to check the water meter?"

∾

Fifteen minutes later, after Morrie had three more brownies and poked and prodded the water meter and pronounced everything 'tickety-boo,' Megan Ingram waved us goodbye from her porch.

Morrie licked his fingers clean as we descended the path. "So Dorothy Ingram wasn't at her sister's when our chair covers were ruined, and she wasn't there tonight. She's been lying. Naughty girl."

"That means she could be our saboteur," I growled. "And she's not finished yet. So much for you solving the problem."

Morrie placed a hand on my shoulder. His touch was firm, strong, determined. His eyes were that icy steel that I'd come to know as a man who fought to control his most chaotic urges. "Then let us solve her together."

CHAPTER 12
MORRIE

We returned to Argleton in another Uber. On the way, I mentally ran over all the methods I had at my disposal to locate and neutralise Dorothy Ingram. Once I'd discarded all the violent options (damn that birdie and his conscience), I had only a handful of methods left.

First, we returned to Nevermore so I could pick up some supplies. Quoth was perched on his favorite swing beside the fireplace, well out of reach of Grimalkin's kittens and their obsession with pulling out his tail feathers.

Mina's sound asleep, he told us as I rummaged around in my desk. *Remember, we're solving this non-violently.*

With my devices in hand, we returned to Dorothy's home under the shadow of night, where I placed a tracking device on her car and a small hidden camera in a tree, pointing at her front door. I pulled up the app and showed Heathcliff the camera feed and a blinking marker on the map.

"We'll be able to keep tabs on her movements. She'll have to take her car if she wants to get back to Lachlan Hall—"

"Sssssh. She's right there," Heathcliff growled, pointing at

Dorothy's house. Sure enough, a light went on in her shed. A few moments later she emerged, her arms loaded down with flower arrangements. Of course, she would be replacing the flowers for the week's church services. But where had she been before, if not at her sister's? Picking up flowers from another parishioner? Late at night? Without her car?

Her garden was a barren stretch of overgrown grass. She wasn't out picking flowers in the moonlight.

Heathcliff and I exchanged a look, and we both took off at a run back towards the church. Behind us, I heard Dorothy close the boot of her car.

"We need to beat her there," I whispered, realizing that we'd have to run the long way around the block. "Let's take a shortcut."

We were directly in front of the row of terraced houses behind the church. I vaulted the low fence that led into the first house, leapt gracefully over a bird bath, and attacked the next fence.

I landed in Maisie's yard, directly in front of the spot where James Pond had been duck-napped. Heathcliff grunted as he came down beside me, his boot getting tangled in the wire of the duck palace.

"Stop flailing around," I hissed as I freed him. We raced across the yard and vaulted the next fence, landing in Stanley's tidy garden. We dodged around an *enormous* birdbath and water feature. From inside the house, I heard a musical tune, like someone whistling, but the whole house was in darkness.

Two more yards, and we made it into the churchyard. Dorothy's car wasn't in the parking lot.

The ancient church lock took me all of thirty-two seconds to pick, and Heathcliff and I snuck inside and hid in the sacristy.

Not three minutes later, the main doors creaked open. I leaned around the sacristy door, observing Dorothy strolling down the aisle, her arms loaded down with floral arrangements. Her permanent frown had mellowed into a shy little smile. She actually looked...happy.

Did Dorothy Ingram know *how* to be happy?

Was she feeling smug because she'd just destroyed our wedding cake?

We were here to find out.

I stepped out of the sacristy. "Hello, Dorothy."

"Get away from me." She swiveled on her heel and made a run for the church doors, scattering flower petals behind her. Heathcliff stepped out from behind the baptismal font and slammed the door shut, blocking her escape with his bulk.

"I'll scream," she yelled, her body taut as she whipped her head between us.

"Go ahead," Heathcliff growled. "You're standing inside a box of medieval stone, and the nearest people are all at the pub, jiving along to the mediocre Saturday night covers band. No one will hear you."

"No one says jiving anymore," I told him sternly. He shot me one of those exasperated Heathcliff looks that made me want to back him up against a wall and shove my tongue down his throat.

But first, the foreplay.

I cracked my knuckles. "We don't want to hurt you, Dorothy. We've come to chat."

"I have nothing to say to you."

"That's funny, because you've been awfully chatty, leaving us a note so that we'd know exactly why you were sabotaging our wedding."

"I didn't write you any note and I don't know what you're talking about. I want as little to do with you as possible."

"The feeling is definitely mutual," Heathcliff growled. "But you're the one trying to sabotage our wedding. I thought Morrie made it clear that if you continue to mess with Mina's special day, we won't hesitate to use our considerable resources to make you stop."

Dorothy folded her arms and glared at us both, although her eyes betrayed a flicker of fear. "I'm sure I don't know what you mean."

"Thou shalt not lie, Dorothy. We know that you've been lying about going to see your sister. So where are you? Up at Lachlan Hall messing with our chair covers?"

"Or in Oliver's kitchen, destroying our cake?"

"It's none of your business where I've been, and I don't have to tell you anything."

I grinned. "But that's not true, is it? Surely you remember the little secret Mina and I uncovered about that baby you secretly got rid of. I wonder if your fellow villagers would like to know the truth—"

"You can't hurt me with that secret," Dorothy sneered. "As soon as I found out that you knew about my shameful decision, I confessed it all in my prayer circle. Everyone already knows. My Lord forgives me for my sins."

Heathcliff's dark eyes narrowed on me. I lifted an eyebrow at him, my mind whirring as I searched for a way to save this situation.

We may not have leverage on Dorothy, but we do have one thing going for us.

We're morally bankrupt and willing to do anything to protect Mina.

"That's not the only secret you're keeping, is it, Dorothy?" I smiled. "You've told Father Clarence and everyone else who will listen that you're looking after your sister, but she told us that she cut you off. Her legs were perfectly fine. So where have you been going on those nights you claim to be the good samaritan?

Nights that *just so happen* to coincide with the destruction of certain elements related to our wedding."

Now that flicker of fear was back in her eyes.

"What I choose to do is none of your business," she snapped. "And as for your wedding, perhaps the Lord is visiting his vengeance upon you for your sins."

"Love is *never* a sin," Heathcliff rasped, his whole body trembling. He was going to lose it in a second.

I placed my hand on his shoulder and gave him a shove toward the doors. "We're watching you."

"I'm not afraid of you," she spat the words. "I answer to a higher power. You don't intimidate me. And just because you shut down my prayer meeting about your blasphemous union doesn't mean that you've seen the last of me."

She tossed the flowers at Heathcliff. He flailed, trying to catch them, and she ducked around him, tugged the door open, and fled into the night.

I picked rose petals out of his beard. "That went well."

"It did not. Now she knows that we have nothing useful on her, and she's got even more motivation for ruining our wedding. And we don't even know if she's the saboteur. It could still be Wayne or someone else."

"Whoever they are, they've already messed up the chair covers and the cake. What's the next big wedding thing that's happening?"

Heathcliff furrowed his brow in thought. "Sixteen boxes of fancy Swiss chocolates are getting delivered tomorrow evening. They're for the wedding favors, provided Helen actually gives us monogrammed bags to put them in."

"Okay, that's good." I rubbed my hands together. "The saboteur won't be able to resist screwing that up. I propose that we lay a trap."

TEXT MESSAGES BETWEEN MORRIE AND MRS. ELLIS

Good evening, Mrs. Ellis. Are you still at the pub?

Of course. The covers band are just finishing up their final set. I'm hoping to go home with the drummer.

I wish you all the best in your amorous endeavours. I wondered if you might be able to help us with something?

As long as it doesn't cut into my shagging time.

I don't think you'll have any trouble. I want you to spread the word around the village that Heathcliff is expecting a shipment of very expensive chocolate tomorrow morning at precisely 10AM at Lachlan Hall, and that he's sent all the security home for the day off, and Cynthia and her staff would be busy all day with the closing ceremony for the National Trust conference on the other end of the estate. I want you to make especially sure that Wayne Bryant and Dorothy Ingram hear about this. Can you do that?

Consider it done.

Done.

Already? Or are you referring to the drummer?

A word of wisdom from your elders, James – don't ask questions for which you do not truly wish to know the answers.

MESSAGE ON NEVERMORE BOOKSHOP SOCIALS

Thank you to everyone who RSVPed for Mina's book launch on the 21st. Due to unforeseen circumstances, this event has been canceled. Copies of Mina's book, *A Dead and Stormy Night*, will no longer be made available. Sorry for any inconvenience caused.

TEXT MESSAGE TO MORRIE FROM HIS SECRET CONTACT WITHIN THE PRISON SYSTEM

James, I have checked over the list of prisoners that you sent me. Can confirm, all still incarcerated. Angus Donahue is currently in solitary after he beat up his cellmate for putting a dead locust in his bunk. I haven't heard of any hits out on your girl. No one would be stupid enough to attempt it. But I'll keep my ear to the ground for you.

Did you hear about that patient who escaped from Crixley? That's up near your way, isn't it? Wild stuff. Where's my wedding invite?

CHAPTER 13

MINA

I was tucked up in bed, trying to sleep, when Morrie returned for something. He and Quoth had a whispered conversation in the hallway. I tried to listen in, but I couldn't hear a thing. Morrie left again, and I pulled my phone out from beneath the blankets and scrolled my emails.

Nothing.

Not one of my invited literary guests had RSVPed to the book launch.

I bit back a flood of tears waiting behind my eyes and typed out a message for my social media. I posted it on my personal page and shared it on Nevermore's pages.

It's done.

A cold wave of grief mixed with relief swept over me. I tossed my phone at the end of the bed. Grimalkin yowled with surprise and jumped down, followed by a line of kittens, all rolling and stomping off in disgust. My grandmother was altogether a bad influence on them.

My fingers brushed the stack of Braille pages on the bedside table. My manuscript. I was supposed to get the final version to the printer this afternoon so they could print off enough copies in time for the launch, but I just couldn't make myself send the file.

The tears spilled over. This was it. This was the end of another dream. If I wasn't supposed to be a writer, then what...

"Mina, what's wrong?"

Quoth's worried voice came from the doorway. A bright shaft of light pierced the gloom – the hallway light shining from our open bedroom door.

"How did you know I was awake?" I rubbed my eyes.

"I could hear your phone talking."

"Right. Of course."

"Mina, what's wrong? You're crying."

"Nothing's wrong." I knew I didn't sound convincing. "I canceled my book launch."

The bed sagged as he laid down beside me, his hand stroking my cheek, his silken hair falling over my shoulder. "But why? You worked so hard to finish your manuscript. And it's perfect. You don't need to re-edit it. All your friends are coming. Why cancel?"

"I know I'm being silly, but I can't help the way I feel." I pressed my cheek into his warm hand. "All week I've had this gnawing sensation in my gut that I was making a huge mistake. Not a single one of the book people I invited is coming, and I think it's because they know my book won't be successful. They're embarrassed by the idea of being associated with me. I can't...I can't bear it. So I'm canceling, at least until I figure out what I'm going to do. Maybe Jen's right, and I should rewrite the book."

Quoth cleared his throat. "I don't think you should cancel."

I sniffed. "It's already done. I just put up the message now."

"Okay. I didn't want to have to do this, but I'm forced to."

He grabbed my hands, tugging me upright.

"What are you doing?"

"On your feet. We're dancing."

"*What?* I'm in my PJs."

"Exactly." His lips brushed the hollow of my neck as he dragged me out of bed. "You're beautiful and I want to dance with you."

Oscar grunted in his sleep, but he didn't make any move to rescue me.

Quoth dragged me into the living room and stood me beside the fireplace while he pushed the chairs out of the way (much to Grimalkin's disdain) and rolled up the rug.

"You're serious about this dancing thing."

"Of course I am. We're getting married in three days, and we have yet to practice for our first dance. And nothing will take your mind off the book launch like a swing around the floor."

"But...you've seen me dance. You know I'm hopeless," I say. "Remember when I kicked Heathcliff's shins raw during the Jane Austen Experience?"

"I'll never forget it," Heathcliff growled from behind me. "You crippled me for life."

I whirled around just as Morrie came up the stairs behind Heathcliff. They both smelled of fresh grass and sweat, as if they'd been running around the village in the moonlight, and I also caught a faint whiff of cake icing.

"You seem to be walking just fine," I said to Heathcliff. "Quoth dragged me out of bed to teach me how to dance."

"Quoth is full of good ideas. I don't want to be hobbled on my wedding day." Heathcliff shrugged off his coat. "Morrie and I will join you."

"I thought you detested dancing?"

"I do, but Morrie made us take lessons," Heathcliff said.

"I didn't want any of you to embarrass me on my wedding day," Morrie said. "That includes you, gorgeous."

"It's *our* wedding day, and I'll have you know that I was

planning to headbang to Rancid and Metallica for the whole night. I am a champion headbanger."

"An excellent plan as always." Morrie took my hand and led me to the center of the room. "But not the plan we're enacting. We are going to wow everyone."

Quoth started the music, a low, crunchy, sexy song. Morrie yanked my arm, spinning me wildly and then capturing my back against his chest, his arms tight around me. He scraped his tongue along my collarbone, raising a trail of goosebumps over my skin.

"They didn't teach you to dance like this in that class you're taking," I whispered.

"The teacher told me to add my own flair." Morrie's lips captured mine, tipping my head back in a deep, sultry kiss as he dipped me lower.

I whimpered as his lips left mine, and he lifted me upright again before turning me in a complex series of steps that had me completely flustered and standing on his toes.

"I thought blind people were supposed to have excellent hearing," Morrie said, because he knew it would annoy me.

"That's a myth, and you know it. Our hearing doesn't magically become superhuman because we lose our sight. We just become more aware of sound. And right now, I'm aware of you being a prat—"

My words cut off as Heathcliff and Quoth pressed themselves against me, their limbs tangling around me.

The three of them held me, turning me around the room with such speed and grace that all I could do was follow where they led. As they spun me, their lips took turns to graze my cheeks, my forehead, my collarbone, until my skin was alight with their caresses and the pulse of the music hummed in my veins.

I imagined us dancing like this on our wedding, all my friends and family watching...

Watching...

Raw panic gripped me, making me stop in my tracks and sending Heathcliff toppling heavily to the floor.

All our wedding guests were invited to the book launch, which I just canceled.

They'd spend the whole wedding asking what happened, and when they watched me dancing, they would whisper that Mina Wilde thought she could be a writer, but how foolish was she?

They would know that I'd failed. Again.

"I can't do this." I gripped Quoth's arm as Heathcliff staggered to his feet.

"You were dancing perfectly fine a moment ago," Morrie pointed out.

"Mina, what is it?" Quoth squeezed my hand.

"It's..." I glanced over my shoulder, which was silly, because no one was there, but I could already feel their pitying eyes on me. "I can't dance in front of everyone at the wedding."

"Don't worry, we won't let you trip," Heathcliff murmured, wrapping a reassuringly heavy arm around my middle.

"It's not that." I leaned back against Quoth's shoulder, shrugging out of Heathcliff's grip. "Everyone is going to know that I'm a failure."

"You're not a failure, Mina." Quoth brushed his lips against the top of my head. "Mina canceled her book launch."

"Gorgeous, *no*. Why did you do that?" Morrie's voice sounded unusually sincere.

"Because I didn't get a single book person interested in my novel. I don't want to put this book out in the world if it's not ready or it's not what people want to read. So I have to keep working." I swallowed down the lump of disappointment. "It's fine. I will keep plugging away at this book until it's perfect. But when I go to the wedding, everyone will know why I canceled. They'll talk about it, about how I was silly for even thinking I could write a book, about how I lost my dream job and now I can't even do this right. They'll laugh at me. They'll *pity* me."

"No one pities you," Heathcliff growled. "I'll have them slowly pecked to death by angry geese if they ever dared."

I smiled through the tears. "I'm so sorry. Here you three are, bending over backwards to make this a perfect wedding for me, taking *dancing* lessons, and I can't get out of my own head enough to appreciate it. I feel *awful*. But there are going to be so many people at the reception, and they will all know that I've failed, and I..."

"No one has to watch you if you don't want them to," Quoth said, his voice dark with determination.

Before I could protest, something warm and feathery grazed my cheek. Quoth spun me around and pressed me against his body, chest to chest, his heart racing against mine.

His body swayed to the music as he jerked a little, holding me tighter. With my head pressed against his chest, I could hear his bones snapping, remaking themselves as a warm blanket settled around my body.

What's going on?

It's as if he's shifting, but I'm still holding him, and there's a warm blanket wrapped around us both...

But how?

The blanket over me rustled, and another feather grazed my arm.

Feathers.

I gasped.

Quoth had enveloped me in his wings.

"What is happening?" I whispered as we kept on swaying.

Inside his wings, the music was muffled, the air in the room pressed in tight by his wings.

"It's a new trick I learned." Quoth sounded so proud. "I can unfurl my wings without transforming completely. It means that they come out Quoth-sized instead of raven-sized."

I rested my cheek against the soft feathers, feeling the membrane beneath them shift as Quoth moved his body in time to the music. Cocooned inside his wings, I felt safe. Nothing could get me in here, neither judgment nor pity.

I let out the breath I'd been holding. "Quoth, this is..."

"If you don't want to dance in front of everyone, you don't have to," he whispered. "But I wish I could show you what you are to me. Mina, you are *amazing*. You wrote a book. Who cares what a bunch of literary snobs think about it?"

"I do," I sniffed. "And I don't know why."

"I think I do," he said, but he didn't elaborate. He only squeezed me tighter.

CHAPTER 14
MINA

I woke up the next morning in Quoth's arms. Heathcliff and Morrie were in the corner of our room, whispering to each other. My ears pricked when I heard the words 'Mrs. Ellis' and 'laid the trap.'

"What's going on?" I sat up.

"Secret wedding stuff," Heathcliff said.

"How is there still wedding stuff that needs doing?" I asked. "We have outfits, food, a brilliant celebrant, and cake. You're going to wear a shirt that's ironed. Morrie's agreed to wear trousers. We're good."

"We're *almost* good," he agreed. "I just need Morrie and Quoth to come to Lachlan Hall with me for a 10AM appointment—"

I made a face. "I was hoping Morrie could help me with a little breaking and entering this morning."

Morrie squeezed my shoulder in approval. "Why, gorgeous, you're speaking my love language."

"*I* need Morrie's unique talents today." I could hear Heathcliff tapping angrily at his phone, which was very odd. Heathcliff didn't like to use his phone at all if it were possible.

Morrie glanced between us. His face softened. "I'm sure that you and Quoth could handle today's project. I've shown you how to use the app."

I raise an eyebrow. *What wedding project could possibly require Heathcliff to use an app?*

Heathcliff made a growling noise, like he was going to argue. "Fine," he sighed. "But if I sound the alarm, you need to come."

~

"WHAT DO YOU SEE?" I hissed at Morrie as I shuffled my weight from foot to foot.

The shrubbery rustled.

Morrie said, "I can see him through the kitchen window. He's sitting at a table, sipping on a cup of tea. Oh, looks as if he's taken a bite of toast. That man takes so long to eat breakfast that I fear the tectonic plates may shift and drop us into the ocean."

I slumped down into a pile of damp, dead leaves and rubbed my aching calves. I'd been hunched in a squat position for what felt like hours, and my body rebelled. Oscar licked my face.

"Surely he has to go somewhere? At some point?"

"He's an old man with what you delightfully referred to as 'resting grump face.' Do you think he has important business meetings to attend? His daily personal training session?"

'Maybe you could stand outside and yell 'fire'?" I suggested.

"Or maybe we should talk about your book launch."

I gritted my teeth. "Quoth already tried that. I don't want to talk about it."

"You have to talk about it. Gorgeous, why did you cancel it? If you'd really wanted those book people to come, I'd have found cruel and creative ways to make that happen—oh, he's moving."

I bolted upright, straining to hear. The door to Stanley's house creaked open, and then I heard him muttering under his breath. A few moments later, a car sped off, the engine backfiring all the way down the road.

Morrie squeezed my hand. "The coast is clear. Let's go."

We crept across the street and strolled up Stanley's well-swept front walk. Morrie rang the bell, whistling a little tune as we waited to see if anyone would answer. When no one did, Morrie positioned himself in front of the door, whistling as he fiddled with the lock.

"I feel like the whole neighborhood is watching me," I said.

"That's because you didn't want to take the time to come up with a convincing disguise. A shame, because the Girl Scout uniform I'd have put you in would look rather fetching...ah." There was a click, and Morrie whispered with an aura of satisfaction, "We have entry."

He walked me and Oscar inside and shut the door softly behind us. The interior of the house was surprisingly light and vibrant. My eyes were drawn to the large windows on the far side of the living room. I instructed Oscar to walk me towards them as Morrie clattered around in Stanley's shoe rack.

"No shoes with a matching tread here, although I suppose he could be wearing them—"

Morrie's voice was drowned out by a chorus of musical notes. I stepped closer to the windows, and the melodious sound filled my ears. My heart lightened as the notes danced in the air, growing louder as—

"Oh, gorgeous, they're absolutely beautiful," Morrie breathed. "There are birds of every color and shape in a huge aviary in front of the windows. It takes up basically the whole living room."

"Wow!" As I stepped closer, I realized I could make out the outline of some of the birds as they flew between their perches and bunched up with their friends. Their voices rose in pitch, some dropping off as others picked up their song. In one corner, I heard a parakeet say, "Crackers n' cheese at 3PM!"

"I can't believe he keeps all these birds inside," I said. "The house doesn't smell at all. He must keep this aviary immaculate."

"It is, and this cage has been custom-built. I remember when we spoke to him at the fence, Stanley said that he liked birds. He wasn't lying."

"But why keep them inside? He could build an aviary in the back yard, and they could be out in the fresh air."

"I'm no bird fancier, but I'm going to guess that an aviary this size might have planning issues." Morrie moved away. "I'm going to check the closets for more shoes. Have a look around in here."

Oscar was so enamoured by the birds that it took me a couple of tries to get him to follow my commands and lead me on a circuit of the room. I found a feeding station and neat boxes filled with bird food, and a set of binoculars resting on the chair beneath the window that faced Maisie's house – the ones Maisie said that she saw him using.

From her house, Maisie wouldn't be able to see the aviary, because it faces the other side of the garden. That's why Morrie didn't notice it when he looked over the fence. She doesn't even know that he has these birds.

I nudged Oscar onward, and he led me to a desk against the wall. I felt around on top. Stanley didn't have a laptop, but there was a pad of paper and pen. When I ran my fingers over the paper, I could feel the indents of the pen. Whatever Stanley was writing, he did it with passion.

"Morrie, can you read this for me?"

Morrie appeared in a flash. He whisked up the letter and read it out in a dramatic tone. "It's a half-finished letter addressed to the parish council from Stanley Clarke. It says, 'I'm writing to you out of concern for the welfare of my neighbor's pet duck, James Pond. I've attempted to bring this matter to the attention of the council on three previous occasions, but in this case, I think the animal inspectors have bird brains if they can't see the issue. I'm not being a crotchety old man. I love birds, and I keep several of my own. My issue is that a drake shouldn't be housed in a residential area, especially not roaming freely the way Ms. Collins does with James in the evenings. It's fair to say that they're not as bad as geese, but a drake can become quite aggressive, and it doesn't look as though Ms. Collins plans to—'"

"Plans to what?"

"I don't know." Morrie flips the paper over. "The letter cuts off. He didn't finish writing it."

"Maybe he didn't feel that he needed to, now that James has gone missing," I said. "We can leave now."

"Leave? But we haven't even started snooping in the bedroom. I bet this guy has a full-sized parrot suit hiding in his closet."

"Stanley Clarke didn't bird-nap James. Look around." I gestured in the direction of the aviary. "Stanley loved birds. He wouldn't hurt a creature. He may have disagreed with how Maisie was raising James Pond, but he's no bird killer—"

Oscar barked.

"Oscar?" He barked again. I raced back to the living room where I'd left him. As a guide dog, Oscar was trained not to bark unless he needed to alert me about something. So I raced to his side. "What is it, buddy?"

Oscar scratched at the window with his paw. He made a whining noise that I'd come to recognise as meaning, 'danger.'

My heart thudded in my chest. "What is it, boy?"

Behind me, Morrie started laughing.

"What? What is it?"

"There's a very large, very round cat strolling across the yard like it owns the place, and it has a huge bird in its mouth."

CHAPTER 15
QUOTH

In line at Ollie's to get our morning coffees, Heathcliff stared at the blinking dot on the tracking app Morrie set up for our main suspect on his phone, and muttered under his breath. Heathcliff muttering wasn't exactly a new thing, but I sensed a tension in him that had to be about Morrie abandoning us to help Mina.

"There are two of us," I said uneasily. "We don't need Morrie for this."

"Hmmmph."

We stepped up to the counter, and I ordered for both of us. I glanced at Heathcliff, but when he didn't look up from his phone, I paid for us both, too, and snuck in a cream doughnut with a big dollop of raspberry jam on top. Mmmm, raspberries. I was *starving*.

"She just appeared on the camera leaving the house." Heathcliff tucked his coffee under his arm as he allowed me to lead him around the tables and out of the shop. "She's dressed in her Sunday best. But is she going to church service? She's getting in her car."

"She only lives two blocks from church," I reminded him.

"Exactly. I think that we split up." Heathcliff tossed his phone at me. I managed to catch it, but not without sloshing hot coffee over myself. "Make that bring me an Uber. I'll go to Lachlan Hall. You follow Dorothy. And text Iwan back. He heard about the chocolate shipment from Mrs. Ellis and he thinks no one will be there to pick it up, so he's offered to head over, since he has something to do. That boy is too useful for his own good."

I stared at the phone. "But how will I contact you?"

He lifted my phone from my pocket. "Problem solved. Now, get going."

I took a long, sad glug of my coffee, then tossed it in a bin as I walked towards the church. People were starting to arrive for the Sunday morning service, but the churchyard was relatively empty. I snuck into the bushes as I navigated the Uber app and called Heathcliff a car. Then, I knelt on the ground and forced my shift. My bones cracked and snapped as my body rearranged itself, and the familiar itchy sensation crawled over my skin as my feathers poked through.

When I was fully bird, I used my beak to pull my clothes into a neat pile, picked up the phone in my talons, and took off. The heavy phone messed with my navigational capabilities, and as I half-soared, half-lurched over the village green, I saw Heathcliff getting into his Uber. I dived for his head, forcing him to dive for safety.

Serves you right for not learning how to use your own phone, I thought.

"I heard that, birdie," he yelled out the window as the car took off.

In my talons, Heathcliff's phone beeped. If I kinked my head to the side, I'd just be able to make out the map of Argleton with the little dot showing Dorothy Ingram's car. She was on the road heading towards Lachlan Hall, but she could be going anywhere. I had to quickly snap my head back as I listed too far to the right and nearly crashed into a power pole.

I'd forgotten to text Iwan before my shift, but we still had twenty minutes before our trap was sprung. I'd be able to text him once I was out of the sky. I checked the map again, flapping my wings harder so I could keep up. Hopefully, Dorothy would stop soon. This phone was heavy, and my flying was erratic and a bit terrifying.

I caught up with her vehicle on Baddesley Road, a long country lane with tall hedgerows on either side. There were another couple of cars a bit further up ahead, possibly delegates or staff for the National Trust conference. I could see Heathcliff's car a little behind hers. Dorothy passed the turnoff to the farm shop, which meant that she had to be heading to Lachlan Hall...

Except that she turned into a narrow country track, her tiny car bumping along the dirt road. The track looked to be part of the woods on the edge of the Lachlan estate. I had to get beneath the tree canopy to follow her, and the phone was now so unbearably burdensome that I settled for landing and dragging it along the ground.

Where is she going?

She came to a locked gate. A sign on the gate read:

PRIVATE PROPERTY. TRESPASSERS WILL BE PROSECUTED
HUNTERS, PLEASE LEAVE WOODS AND GATES AS YOU
FIND THEM

I hid in the bushes and watched Dorothy Ingram get out of her car, unlock the gate, and shut it behind her before driving on.

The phone vibrated in my talons. Someone was calling. It was probably Heathcliff trying to call me to tell me he'd made it to the hall. I drew back behind Dorothy's car so she wouldn't hear it.

After a couple of miles, Dorothy pulled into a small clearing in front of a dilapidated hunting bothy. A second car was already parked beside it, but I didn't recognize it. I watched Dorothy get out and go up to the door of the bothy. She had a key for it, too. She let herself inside.

A moment later, I could hear her voice, raised with concern. It sounded as though she was talking to someone, although I couldn't hear their voice.

Something was wrong.

The phone vibrated again. I dragged it even further back into the woods, in time to see Dorothy flee from the bothy and back into her car. I forced my shift and huddled, naked, beneath an old oak and picked up the phone. My own name flashed across the screen. Heathcliff.

I pressed it to my ear. "I followed Dorothy to this old hunting bothy in the woods on the Lachlan estate, but—"

"Never mind that," Heathcliff snapped. "I'm in the loading bay now. We have a problem."

My chest clenched. "Has the saboteur struck again?"

"It's Iwan. I just tripped over his body. He's been hit over the head by your large decorative urn, and he's not breathing."

CHAPTER 16
MORRIE

Oscar pawed at the window again. He looked over at the cage, where the birds were twittering excitedly. They'd seen the cat, too. Oscar touched his paw to Mina again, but looked over at me, as if to say, "Help me. I can't save them all."

"I think Oscar might be trying to protect the birds from that cat," I told Mina. "He can see that you like the birds, so he's letting you know about a danger to them."

"Oh, Oscar, you're so clever." Mina chewed her lip in that way she did when she was thinking. "I wonder...do you think a cat could have made the hole in James' pen?"

"A normal cat? Probably not. But the cat outside is no ordinary feline." I winced as the cat crunched happily on its quarry, breaking the neck with one ruthless bite. Thankfully, the unfortunate victim wasn't a duck. "He's the cat equivalent of Heathcliff, only even more handsome. Why? What are you thinking?"

"I'm wondering if maybe we shouldn't be looking at a human culprit for our bird-napping crime. If that cat got James, he might have brought some piece of him back to his owner, the way Grimalkin delights us with her little presents of bird guts on the staircase."

"Don't remind me. Last time Heathcliff trod on one, he wailed at a pitch that would make dogs cry."

"If we find the owner, we might at least learn the fate of our poor duck." Mina thrusted her fist in the air. "Follow that cat!"

I raced outside, Mina and Oscar hot on my heels. I vaulted over the garden fence into Maisie's yard, but the cat was already dancing along the top of the fence on the other side. By the time I'd navigated my way around James Pond's empty duck mansion, the cat was two houses away.

I noticed that Heathcliff and I had left deep bootprints in the mud next to the duck-napper's bootprint from our adventure vaulting the fences the other night.

"Oh, no you don't. I'm the greatest criminal mastermind that ever existed, inside and outside of fiction. You won't escape me." I shoved myself up onto the fence just in time to see the cat rocket across a garden two away from me and disappear through a cat door.

"Aha! So that's your home, is it, you foul beast?" I hauled my weary body over the penultimate fence and dropped over the other side.

Straight into a holly hedge.

Ow.

"Ow!"

Ow. Owie. *Ow.*

"Are you okay?" Mina yelled from Stanley's garden.

I winched as I tugged a long thorn from my arm. "I feel like I've just tried to make love to a porcupine."

"You'll be fine, greatest criminal mastermind of all fiction. Find that cat!"

The damn cat. Right. I limped across the next garden, leaving a trail of holly thorns in my wake. Luckily, the two houses had a gate between them, so I didn't have to vault another fence. I made it to the cat's home without any more disasters befalling me.

The cat door was located on a narrow porch, and along the end of the porch was a narrow, muddy path. It looked as though the owner had been laying fresh pavers but hadn't quite made it to the porch.

"Meorrrw!"

The cat shook its quarry, mocking me from behind the glass.

I growled, baring my teeth as I leapt over the mud. As I landed on my feet beside a huge pile of mismatched shoes, I noticed the imprint of a boot in the mud.

Aha.

The cat forgotten, I bent down to examine the footprint carefully. The tread was exactly the same as the footprint we found at the scene of the duck-napping.

Which was *also* the same boot that I'd seen in the cemetery the night we followed Wayne Bryant. Whoever was in Maisie's garden was also here, and judging by the way the trail of prints left the house and went around to the side gate, I suspect I found the duck-napper's home.

"Meow!" The cat batted what remained of his quarry around the sitting room, like some sort of grisly sports game of which only he understood the rules. I watched him, my mind whirring.

No one came to stop the cat. Either the inhabitants of the home were sadistic villains who enjoyed watching the torture of animals (always a possibility) or no one was home. Good, that gave me ample snooping time.

I checked all the shoes in the pile, but couldn't find a set that matched the tread. That probably meant that wherever the duck-napper was now, they were probably wearing their shoes.

Then, I noticed a corner of the garden bed where the dirt

had been disturbed by recent digging. A small trowel was stuck in the dirt. It was the wrong time of year for planting bulbs, and given the garden's proximity to the cat door, and the cat's obvious proclivities, I deduced that the bed was used by the cat's minions for burying its quarry.

I grabbed the trowel gingerly, for these hands were not made for manual labour, and scraped back the dirt, uncovering a couple of rat carcasses and the remains of several distinctive birds, but no duck.

Unless he ate all the evidence (unlikely, I've seen photographs of James Pond. That duck was chonky), or left the remains in someone else's garden, the cat wasn't our killer.

But whoever lives in this house was *in Maisie's garden.*

Now all we needed to do was figure out who lived here.

I picked a path around the side of the house, avoiding sinking my Brionis into the mud, and ended up on the short driveway. My dark heart pattered as I recognised the large farm vehicle parked in the driveway with 'Wayne Bryant: Veterinarian' painted on the side.

This house belongs to Wayne Bryant, the writer we are investigating for sabotaging our wedding.

And although his work vehicle is here, he's not home right now.

I was just debating whether to entertain another round of breaking and entering when I heard Mina call my name. Her voice sounded frantic.

"Coming, gorgeous!" I took off down the street. When I rounded Stanley's driveway, my heart stuttered. Stanley held a struggling Mina by the wrist, his eyes narrowed while he tried to fight off a distraught Oscar with his foot.

"Morrie, help!" Mina cried.

"Put her down." I didn't raise my voice. I didn't have to. Years of bossing around lackeys had shown me how to drip malice from every syllable.

Stanley released Mina. His gaze flicked from me to her, his jaw trembling.

"I recognise you two. You were at Maisie Collins' home the other day. What were you doing in my house?" He narrowed his eyes. "I'm calling the police. This is harassment."

"Please don't," Mina cried.

"Sir, we apologize for causing any distress. Mina and I are merely concerned citizens," I said, thinking fast. "We were walking by on our way to visit Maisie, and we happened to notice your door was unlocked. We went inside to check that there hadn't been some kind of medical emergency, then I went down the street to see if I could spot you, while Mina waited here, guarding the door."

"I'd hardly be burgling anyone," Mina said with a laugh, clutching Oscar's harness. "How would I even know where to find your valuables?"

Oh, be still my heart. My girl is too good at this.

Stanley's face softened as he took in Mina and Oscar. "Well, thank you for looking out for me. It's good to know that I have nice neighbors like you around. Most people aren't so nice. They think that I'm grumpy and don't want to talk to me. They're probably right."

"I think that if they got to know you, they'd change their minds." Mina beamed her beautiful smile. "I found all those birds you have in your indoor aviary, and your bird-watching binoculars. You care a great deal about birds, don't you?"

"They are such beautiful creatures. They deserve good treatment. I am sorry that Maisie lost her companion. I hope you find him."

With that, he went inside and closed the door.

I slid Mina's hand through my arm and led her away. "You won't believe what I discovered—"

"I'm sure it's very interesting, Morrie, but we have to check

Maisie's house," she hissed. "When Stanley caught me, he came from her front garden. I heard his feet crunching on the gravel on her driveway."

We walked over to Maisie's. There were no windows broken or duck-related graffiti sprayed on the walls. I was about to give up when I noticed something beside the front door.

"He left her a gift." On the porch was a bunch of yellow flowers that had been thoughtfully chosen to perfectly match James Pond's feathers, and a small card with a smiling duck on the cover. I opened the card. There, in the same handwriting he'd used to pen that note to the council, Stanley had written:

DEAR MAISIE,
I'M DUCKING SORRY FOR YOUR LOSS.
SINCERELY, STANLEY.

"Okay, so it *definitely* wasn't Stanley." I tugged Mina back down the driveway. "But I've found another lead. You know the footprint we found beside James Pond's pen? I found the same footprint—"

My phone buzzed in my pocket. Heathcliff's ringtone. Heathcliff wouldn't use his phone unless something had gone wrong with their trap.

Heart pounding against my chest, I stopped in the footpath and brought the phone to my ear. "Let me guess, you forgot which app to use and have accidentally ordered seventeen pizzas?"

"Are you with Mina?" Quoth's voice startled me. He was whispering. "You have to come to Lachlan Hall right away."

"Why are you whispering?"

"Because I'm stark naked and hiding in the bushes, is why."

"And why are you stark naked and hiding in the bushes with Heathcliff's phone?"

Mina's head snapped to me, her eyes wide with fear.

"Because I'm hiding from the police. Heathcliff found Iwan's body. He's been murdered."

CHAPTER 17
MINA

Murdered? Our beautiful celebrant? But...*why?*

How could a murder happen so close to our wedding?

"Arf?" Oscar sounded as distressed as I felt.

Morrie listened to Quoth for a few more moments, then rang off. He tugged my hand in the direction of Nevermore Bookshop. "We need to get back to the shop and bring Quoth a change of clothes. He left his in the woods behind the graveyard after Heathcliff told him to follow Dorothy Ingram. I'll call an Uber from there."

"Wait, why did *Heathcliff* want Quoth to follow Dorothy Ingram?"

"Oh. Er. Secret wedding stuff." Morrie practically dragged me and Oscar down the street. "And that's the only answer you'll get out of me."

My stomach twisted in knots as we jogged back to Nevermore. I ran up to Quoth's bedroom and shoved a random assortment of his clothing into a tote bag, then Oscar and I settled ourselves into the back of an Uber (luckily, the driver, Tamsyn, was a regular, and understood about service animals).

Poor Iwan. He was such a bright, kind-hearted soul. I can't believe someone wanted him dead.

Eight minutes later, we pulled into the long driveway at Lachlan Hall. I'd been here enough times that even though it was pitch black to me outside, I could recognise the change from the rough country road to the effortlessly smooth concrete and the soft crunch as the car drove over dropped acorns from the towering oaks that lined the long driveway.

As Tamsyn came to a stop, I noticed blinking lights all around us. Police cars, ambulances, and people scurried about. It was a lot of stimulation for my eyes, and I slid gingerly out of the car, gripping Oscar's harness tight as a bright orange light flickered across my vision and the beginning of a migraine flared in my temple.

"There you are," Heathcliff's voice boomed. Instantly, I felt better. *Heathcliff's alive. He's okay.*

A moment later, he pulled me into his arms, crushing me against him. "Don't worry, Mina. It will be okay. You're safe with me."

"Of course I am." I squeezed him extra tight. "I'm not the one who found a murder scene. Tell me what happened?"

"I was here, waiting for a delivery of secret wedding stuff. It was only me, because I gave the security team the day off and Cynthia was busy with the conference. I heard something around the side of the house. I came around and found Iwan lying there, his head bashed in, and one of Quoth's decorative urn props beside him, covered in blood. I called the police and looked around for a murderer, but there are a million places to hide in this place."

"Have you seen Quoth?"

"I called him as soon as I found Iwan. Quoth flew over immediately. I've seen him fly overhead a couple of times, so I assume he's hiding somewhere nearby. Come on." Heathcliff started leading me back to the car. "Let's get you home. What I could do with right now is a—"

"Heathcliff Earnshaw," DS Wilson's authoritative voice cut through me like a knife. "I don't know where you think you're going. We need to talk to you."

Heathcliff's body tensed. "I've given a statement."

"Yes, you have. But that was before we found this on the victim's phone." She held out an object. "You can see it in this photo I'm showing you now."

"What is it?" I asked, leaning in, even though it was unlikely I'd see anything. I could discern that we were all looking at her phone.

Wilson said triumphantly. "It's a text message, sent from one Heathcliff Earnshaw, demanding the victim meet him in the exact spot where he was murdered."

CHAPTER 18

MINA

hat?

That doesn't make any sense.

"I never sent that text message," Heathcliff growled. "I don't send text messages."

"It's true," I explained. "It took six months to wear him down enough to join a group chat with me and Quoth and Morrie, and he only uses it when he wants one of us to come and rescue him from a customer. Heathcliff either ignores people or calls them so that they can *hear* his disdain."

"Then how do you explain this text?" Wilson tapped her phone screen.

"Isn't that *your* job?" Heathcliff snapped.

I placed my hand on his arm, wishing I could communicate with him telepathically the way I could with Quoth and tell him that talking back to DS Wilson was probably not in his best interests.

Don't you think I haven't tried, Quoth's deep, raven voice echoed between my ears. He must be nearby in the bushes. *Even if he could read your thoughts, he wouldn't listen.*

Wilson folded her arms. "I'll need you to come to the station for questioning. Do you have your phone with you?"

"No. That's why this doesn't make sense. I accidentally picked up Allan's phone this morning, and he has mine."

"Uh-huh, sure." Wilson didn't sound as if she believed him. I guess she heard that kind of excuse all the time. But I knew Quoth had Heathcliff's phone because he called Morrie on it, but I didn't understand *why. What was this secret wedding stuff Heathcliff and Quoth were up to?* "We'll need to speak with Allan, as well. Will you follow me to my car, or do I need to get a couple of officers over here?"

"I'm coming." Heathcliff gave my hand a squeeze. "Mina, please don't worry. I didn't commit this crime or send that text. We'll get this straightened out and I'll be back to marry you before you know it."

His hand slipped away as he followed Wilson to her car.

My stomach churned. *How can this be happening?*

When I woke up this morning, the worst thing in my life was that I had to stick a second sign on the front door of Nevermore Bookshop announcing that my book launch was canceled. But now a wonderful man was dead and my fiancé was suspected of murdering him.

A sick sensation churned in my stomach. It was true that I found myself in the middle of murders more times than the usual person, but it didn't make them any easier. Iwan was our friend, and now he was *gone.* And I wanted to do whatever I could to help bring his killer to justice.

But that probably meant finding out what my three fictional fiancés were getting up to in secret.

Behind me, Morrie tossed the tote bag containing Quoth's clothes over a box hedge. I heard a raven croak, and a few moments later, Quoth emerged and wrapped his arms around me. I felt the prickle against my skin as his feathers threatened to burst through the surface. He was upset, too.

"It's all my fault," he whispered. "Heathcliff told me to text Iwan and tell him not to worry about the chocolate delivery. That's why I had his phone. But in all the chaos, I forgot. If I'd just sent that text, Iwan wouldn't have come here—"

"Did you hear what the police said? Heathcliff *did* text Iwan, telling him that he was going to meet him here."

"That's not true." Quoth held me tighter. "I had Heathcliff's phone, and I didn't send a text to Iwan. Oh, what a horrible mess. I'll go to the station and explain everything."

"Quoth, what did happen?"

"I came here as soon as Heathcliff called me," he whispered to me. "The police were already here when I arrived. Apparently, they'd had a tipoff about Heathcliff having an altercation with someone at Lachlan Hall. But that's not true."

The killer called the police. Whoever they were, they didn't merely want Iwan dead, they wanted to frame Heathcliff.

"I don't understand any of this." I turned to Morrie and Quoth. "Why would anyone want to kill Iwan to frame Heathcliff? Do you guys know anything about this? Has it got something to do with all this secret wedding stuff?"

There were three beats of silence, during which time a thousand dark thoughts ran through my mind. Then Morrie said, "I don't think Heathcliff's taste for imported chocolates or over-the-top wedding decor are anything to get a murderer worked up about. It's more likely that this is about Iwan, some dark secret he was hiding, and the killer is looking to make Heathcliff take the fall so the police stop looking for them."

Quoth nuzzled his face into my shoulder, and said nothing.

"The police will quickly figure out that our favorite Luddite couldn't have sent those texts once we show them his phone,"

Morrie tried to reassure me. "Then they can focus on finding the real killer—"

"But then *who* could have sent those texts? They must have some kind of tech knowledge to convince Iwan that they were Heathcliff. If we hurry back to Nevermore Bookshop and Morrie checks over Heathcliff's phone before the police come for it, maybe we can figure out how they did it and—"

"Oh no," Morrie said. "Quoth, don't let her go or she'll run headfirst into a new murder investigation."

"You mean you *don't* want to know what's going on? This is *important.*" My voice cracked. "They think Heathcliff did this!"

"This isn't our fight, gorgeous. We'll get Heathcliff out of this, and Hayes and Wilson will get to the bottom of Iwan's murder. You already have a case, remember? The missing duck. And we're getting married in two days—"

"Are we?" I snapped, a hint of bitterness creeping into my voice.

I was starting to resent all this secret-keeping around the wedding. I was excited that Heathcliff wanted to surprise me, but that was before our celebrant was murdered. Now, it made me feel as if the guys were deliberately keeping me in the dark, like they didn't trust me.

And that gave me a similar squirmy sensation to how I felt when I read Jen's letter about my book.

"Of course, gorgeous. It won't take the police long to clear Heathcliff's name. As long as we cooperate with them, I'm sure everything will be fine and that this has nothing to do with us. It's probably something sordid in Iwan's past."

"I can't imagine Iwan having anything sordid in his past." Iwan was a beloved member of the community – a parish council member, and on the school board. Sure, he might have annoyed a few religious busybodies like Dorothy Ingram by campaigning for gay marriage, but from what I'd seen, since the law had changed and no one had been struck down by a lightning bolt for their 'sinful union,' most villagers seemed happy to let people who were in love get married no matter what sex or gender they might be.

Morrie patted my arm and led me back towards the waiting Uber. "Take my word for it. Everyone has skeletons in their closet."

"You've spent most of your life hanging around criminals. I think you have a skewed sample."

"I agree with Morrie." Quoth pulled me into the back seat behind him, never letting me go for a moment. His voice wavered a little. "We have to let the police handle this one."

"But how can we? They have Heathcliff in custody! And we don't have a celebrant! I wanted Iwan to marry us! I don't feel right having the wedding."

Panic rose in my chest. I'd been taking it for granted that on the 20th, I'd get to marry the three men of my dreams. But now...

"Heathcliff is just answering questions. And Iwan would have wanted us to go on with the wedding."

"But it took us forever to find someone who would agree to perform our ceremony." Marrying four people wasn't legal in the UK, so our ceremony couldn't be legalised, but we wanted to host one anyway. "I'm sorry, I know that's not what matters right now. Poor Iwan. I just feel so helpless. You guys haven't noticed anything strange about the wedding prep? Any clues that someone might be targeting Iwan, or us?"

There was another long beat of silence that made my chest tighten before Morrie replied, "Nope, we're as shocked as you are. But don't worry, we'll get you home and help you forget all about this...for an orgasm or two, at least."

CHAPTER 19

MINA

Heathcliff didn't come home from the police station that night.

The next morning, I woke in a tangle of limbs, but when I felt around Morrie and Quoth's sleeping forms, there was a huge, cold expense of bed real estate where my grumpy antihero normally slept.

Still empty.

Panic rose in my chest. I drew Heathcliff's dressing gown around me, breathing in his fresh, mossy, peaty scent, the scent that lingered from his time on the moors. I stole into the living room and collapsed into his chair beside the dead fire, wincing as I pulled a whisky bottle from behind my bottom.

Heathcliff, please be okay. Please come home to me.

I *knew* that Heathcliff was no murderer – not *this* version of him, anyway. My Heathcliff was so much more than who he was in his book. He was passionate, true-hearted, and loyal, and he cared deeply about people and animals and wild places. And wedding planning, for some reason.

But because of his mysterious past and the way he acted (and probably because of his heritage, because let's be honest, unconscious bias is a thing), people in the village would always assume the worst of him. If Hayes and Wilson were convinced he killed Iwan, they wouldn't bother to search for the real killer. I'd seen it before. I had to—

"Stop thinking what you're thinking," Morrie scolded me as he placed my morning cup of tea into my hands.

"How do you know what I'm thinking?" I sipped the tea. He'd made it perfectly. Of course he had.

"Because I know how your mind works, my brave and determined lady. But we can't do anything."

"There's *plenty* we can do. We can go back to the scene of the crime and look for clues that the police missed. I can talk to Jo and see what she'll tell me about the body, see if there's a clue there, and you can dig into Iwan's past and—"

"Mina, we're not going to do any of that. *We* are going to get married."

"We can't get married if Heathcliff's in jail and our celebrant is dead!"

Morrie sighed. "Quoth will go to the police station and see what he can find out. Won't you?"

Of course, Quoth's voice landed inside my head as he flew into the room. *I know all the sneaky ways to get inside the station now. And Hayes often has a bowl of nuts on his desk.*

Morrie opened the kitchen window, and Quoth dove outside. As he shut the window again, he said, "Why don't you work on your book? That'll take your mind off Heathcliff. I'll even help you. What changes do you want to make?"

My face screwed up.

"Gorgeous, why are you so determined to believe that your story isn't good enough just the way it is?" Morrie knelt down in front of me, his hands brushing my thighs in a way that made my cheeks flush with heat. "Is this why you told that girl you'd find her wayward duck, because you don't want to—"

"James Pond! Of course!" I grabbed Morrie's shoulder. "If I can't work on solving Iwan's murder and clearing Heathcliff's name, then I can at least find Maisie's duck."

If I can do one thing right, at least I'll know that I'm not useless.

"If that's what you really want to do, then I'll help you."

"I want to look for Iwan's murderer, but you're all being stubborn about that." I made a face. "So we're going to find out what happened to James Pond. Yesterday, before we got the phone call from Quoth, you said you had something to show me."

Morrie explained that he'd found a footprint that matched the one we found beside James Pond's pen...at Wayne Bryant's house. "I think that we need to go and ask Wayne some questions."

CHAPTER 20

MINA

After Oscar had his kibble, I put on his harness and he and Morrie and I locked up and headed across the village green. As we walked, Morrie explained to me that the other night when he'd been out on secret wedding business, he'd found *another* footprint in the churchyard near the groundskeeper's shed.

What secret wedding business took you into the churchyard in the middle of the night?

I bit my tongue, because Heathcliff was in *jail* and Morrie would just say that he couldn't tell me anything without getting the okay from the wedding planner. But I didn't like it, not at all.

"Let's go have a look." I pushed open the lychgate and directed Oscar through the overgrown cemetery, remembering that it wasn't too long ago that we'd solved the murders of Jo's girlfriend Fiona and another girl named Jenna who were killed in the cemetery. Our feet crunched over a circle of charred earth where Dorothy Ingram and her Defense against Immorality, Adultery, Bestiality, Lucifer and the Occult group tried to burn a bunch of rare books and held a gun to my head.

I *really* didn't like that woman.

Morrie led me and Oscar over to the groundskeeper's shed. He bent to examine the ground. "The footprint was right over here…interesting."

"What's interesting?"

"It's gone now, of course, but I see *new* footprints – the same herringbone pattern. Wayne came through here, and he's not alone. Someone else walked here, wearing a small, square-heeled, pointed-toe shoe. A woman. Gorgeous, these prints are recent. *Very* recent. As in, they must've been made within the last half hour."

My heart raced. "Can you trace their path?"

"Luckily, we had rain last night, so the ground is damp. Although it's not lucky for my Brionis. Wait here for me." Morrie squelched his way around the churchyard, then returned to me. "I offer you my deductions based on my ex's lessons on studying footprints. Wayne climbed over the fence from that row of townhouses behind the church, and this woman walked into the cemetery from the village green. They both converged on the groundskeeper's hut." He lowered his voice to a whisper. "Their prints go in, but they don't come out."

Morrie tried to peer in the windows, but he said that he couldn't see anything except a pile of blankets. He jiggled the lock. While he set about picking it, I pressed my ear to the door and heard scrambling inside. Someone whispered, "Ooooh, yes, baby, right there…"

"Morrie," I laughed. "There are two people having *sex* in there."

"There are *not*." Morrie pressed his ear to the door. "Oh, you're right. How deliciously sacrilegious. Give me a moment here with the lock…ah!"

The door fell open. Morrie, Oscar and I crashed into the room.

"Argh!"

"What do you think you're doing?"

"Arf arf arf!"

Some object sailed past my ear.

Morrie cracked up laughing. "Oh, gorgeous, you're going to *love* this. Beneath the pile of blankets in the corner are two very red-faced, *very* naked people. Wayne Bryant...and Dorothy Ingram."

"What?"

I couldn't believe it. The idea was *ludicrous*.

Dorothy Ingram wouldn't have a secret tryst with anyone. I'm pretty sure she thought the very act of sex itself was immoral and should be reserved only for making babies. And Wayne was married to the lovely, patient Nora. Why would he sneak around behind her back...with *Dorothy*?

But Morrie was laughing so hard that he was choking, so it must be true.

"So this is the big secret that you've been keeping, Dorothy?" Morrie asked between gasps. "You told everyone that you've been looking after your sister in Grimdale to account for your absence when all the while, you and Wayne have been sneaking off for the Battle of Balls Deep."

I couldn't help laughing at that.

"Get off my shirt, you fool," Dorothy Ingram snapped at her paramour as they struggled to hide themselves.

"Well, maybe if *you* got your claws out of my arm, I could stop being in excruciating pain long enough to help you."

"You know, you don't have to worry about your clothes," I said. "I'm blind, so I can't see you, and Morrie here has seen much more salacious things in his life than a couple of people fucking in the groundskeeper's shed."

"We were not *fucking*," Dorothy spat. "How dare you... you..."

"She's right, Dor," Wayne said. "We were fucking like rabbits, and now Mina Wilde knows our secret, and she's going to take great pleasure in spreading it all over the village. She'll probably put it in the introduction of her book, make sure everyone gets a copy of it on her book launch—"

"I canceled my book launch," I said, the words tasting like dirt. "And I don't see why you're mad at me when *you're* the one cheating on your wife."

"What do you want to keep this secret?" Dorothy asked, her voice dripping with ice.

"Nothing much. Mina only wants to ask you something, and she requires a truthful answer." Morrie nudged my arm. "Go ahead, gorgeous."

"We found your footprint in Maisie Collins' garden," I said. "Right next to where someone cut a hole in a cage and took her prizewinning duck, James Pond. You wouldn't know anything about that, would you?"

"So that's why I haven't heard that incessant quacking at all hours?" Wayne grumbled. "No, I didn't take Maisie's duck. I sneak through the back gardens to come here to see Dorothy so that no one sees me on the street. That's probably how my foot-print got there. We've been meeting here for...for weeks now."

"Oh." I believed them. I mean, we *did* find them in here, naked. And they'd done a great job of sneaking around. Not even Mrs. Ellis had caught on to this juicy village gossip.

But if Wayne didn't duck-nap James, I was back to square one again.

"What about your cat?" I asked Wayne. Morrie had said that he hadn't found duck remains in Wayne's garden, but I knew from my grandmother's stories that cats would often leave their kills in other locations around the village to show off to other cats. "He seems to enjoy birds, and he's big and tough. He could break open a cage if he was determined enough. Have you seen him with any duck feathers?"

"Hercules? No, but I don't exactly track his movements, do I? He's a cat. He comes and goes as he pleases—"

Just then, a flapping noise landed on the roof, followed by some footsteps outside.

Mina, Mina, Quoth called inside my head. *Heathcliff's out of jail! They figured out the text messages didn't even come from his phone, they were just made to look like they did—*

"What's going on in here?" Heathcliff's voice boomed behind me.

I threw myself at him, landing hard against the solid wall of muscle that was his chest. He cried out in surprise, but his arms went around me and he tipped my chin back and crushed his mouth to mine.

The whole world stilled around me, all the worry and fear of the last few days becoming a meaningless hum far, far away as Heathcliff's lips slanted over mine. One of his hands tangled in my hair while the other slid down the curve of my arse. He tasted of wild places and dark, wanton thoughts, and when he parted my lips and slid his tongue over mine, I made a sound that was every bit as debauched as what Dorothy and Wayne were doing.

For days, I'd been worrying that I wasn't good enough, but the way Heathcliff kissed me made me feel as if I didn't have to be anything, that I was all he ever wanted, just the way I was.

"I missed you," Heathcliff growled against my lips.

"Hey, Heathcliff's here," Morrie said.

"Goody," Wayne muttered.

"Save some sugar for me, big guy."

"Croak," Quoth added from his perch on the roof.

"Arf?" Oscar circled my feet.

I broke the kiss to bury my face into his shoulder. His peaty, spicy scent was tinged with the grubby concrete of the cells – a smell I was unfortunately all too familiar with from our numerous brushes with the Argleton police department. "I'm so happy you're back."

"Why are Wayne and Dorothy half-dressed inside the groundskeeper's shed?" Heathcliff peered over my shoulder.

"That's an excellent question, my friend," Morrie said. "One that deserves a detailed response. But right now, we should probably get on to that urgent secret wedding business, shouldn't we?"

Three beats of silence.

Doubt gnawed at my stomach.

"Yes," Heathcliff said slowly. "Quoth, why don't you take Mina back home? Morrie and I have some secret wedding business to do."

"Croak."

A moment later, I felt Quoth's talons sink gently against my shoulder. I nuzzled his feathers. I didn't want to leave Heathcliff, but he was already moving towards Morrie. The doubt inside me became a roar. Why did they still have secrets from me?

But I wasn't going to talk about it in front of Dorothy and Wayne. Besides, I'd gotten my answer. Wayne wasn't our ducknapper. Now I had to think of a new angle.

"Okay, let's go home. I'll see you both later." I shot Morrie what I hoped was a withering glare. "We've got a lot to talk about."

Mina, are you okay? Quoth asked as I stormed back across the square.

"No, I'm not okay. Someone killed Iwan and tried to frame Heathcliff, and the three of you are hiding things from me. Don't get your feathers in a knot. I won't make you tell me and risk incurring the wrath of Heathcliff. But they want me out of the way for whatever reason. Well, *fine*. I still have a case to solve, and one more avenue of investigation open to me. We need to interrogate Hercules, and I know just the agent for the job."

"Let me get this straight," My grandmother crossed her elegant ankles in front of the fire and ran her fingers through her silken black hair. "You want me, a nymph, an actual *half-goddess*, to stalk through the neighborhood after some randy tomcat?"

"If all that yowling under our window and the litter of kittens underfoot are any indication, you *like* randy tomcats."

"Excuse me, but I'm spoken for." Grimalkin pointed to the bright red bauble hanging from her new jeweled collar, which became a choker around her neck whenever she transformed. "What boon will you give me in exchange for this favor?"

"Can't you do it out of the goodness of your heart?"

"I'm a cat, darling. I have no heart."

Sighing, I opened my purse and placed one tin of the fanciest shredded salmon on the table beside her. When my grandmother made no noise, I added a second can.

She sighed. "Fine. But don't make a habit of this. I have my dignity to maintain."

With that, Grimalkin shrank into her clothes. A moment

later, her tailored dress and wedge-heeled boots crumpled to the floor, and a sleek black cat darted out from beneath them.

A moment later, the cat door jangled. Quoth, back in his human form, moved to the window to watch. "There she goes. I bet it won't take her long at all to get to the bottom of this."

"I hope so." I sank down in Heathcliff's chair, feeling about a foot tall. So far, I'd proven myself a complete failure at locating James Pond. Maisie was still worried sick. I invited her to our wedding in the hopes of cheering her up a little, but I knew I'd let her down.

But if Grimalkin could help us find out what happened, then maybe I could prove that I could still be a useful, creative, clever person, and rid myself of this wretched feeling of dread in the pit of my stomach.

CHAPTER 22

HEATHCLIFF

Morrie and I watched Mina stride off across the graveyard with Oscar at her side and Quoth on her shoulder. I could sense that she was annoyed at all this 'secret wedding business,' but there was no way I'd get her involved in our quest to find the saboteur.

When they were safely out of earshot, we turned to each other. Morrie's villainous smile tugged at the edges of his mouth.

Wayne tried to push his way out the door, but I blocked it with my body.

I cracked my knuckles.

"Now that we're alone," Morrie said, "the two of you need to come clean about a few things."

"We don't need to do anything for you." Wayne glared at both of us, but it was ruined by the tremble in his fingers as he grabbed Dorothy's wrist and tried to ram me. He glanced off my chest and fell back into a stack of gardening implements. I barely felt a thing.

"I have spent the night in jail. I'm in no mood to mess about," I growled. "Someone has been sabotaging our wedding, intercepting chair cover deliveries, destroying our wedding cake, and leaving threatening notes addressed to Mina. Whoever did this killed Iwan and left the same kind of note on his body. And we want to know what you two know about it."

"Nothing!" Wayne cried.

"I already told you that I have nothing to do with any of that," Dorothy said.

"Then why did you drive to a secret bothy behind the Lachlan estate right when the murder went down, and then leave in a hurry? The two of you were in it together, weren't you? You hate Mina and you'd do anything to destroy her happiness, even murder an innocent man—"

"We had nothing to do with Iwan's death," Dorothy spluttered. "Tell them, Wayne. I can't bear it any longer!"

She threw herself down in the blankets and buried her face in her hands.

Wayne picked himself up, rubbed a cut on his arm from an inappropriately-hung rake, and went over to her. He rubbed Dorothy's shoulders as his eyes met mine. The fight had left him. He looked resigned and very, very afraid.

Good.

"You have to understand. I love my Nora, but she's so involved in her knitting circle and running around with her friends, I've been feeling like I don't matter to her. I thought I'd get a hobby of my own, so I joined DIABLO—"

"Please don't call it that," Dorothy scolded him. "We're the Defense against Immorality, Adultery, Bestiality, Lucifer and the Occult."

"—and one thing led to another, and Dorothy and I..." Wayne swallowed. "Well, you know. As I said, Dorothy and I have been sneaking into this shed every chance we got. I told Nora that I was off hunting, and Dorothy told anyone who asked that she was looking after her sister. No one has guessed the truth until now, although you actually came close to catching us two nights ago."

"They were *under* the blankets!" Morrie's eyes gleamed at me. "Of course!"

"After that close call, we decided to find a new meeting place," Dorothy said. "Wayne does some hunting in the woods on the Lachlan estate. Deer control, that kind of thing. They have a small bothy that he uses sometimes if he stays the night. He gave me a key to the bothy, and another key for the gate on the road. We went up there to try it out yesterday morning. We heard from Mabel that you had some sort of important delivery up at Lachlan Hall, so we figured you wouldn't be around to harass us."

"I arrived at the bothy first," Wayne said. "I left my work van at home – too easy for someone to spot me – and took Nora's runabout. I wanted to set it up all romantic for Dorothy. I had candles, nice sheets, a little cheese platter..."

Dorothy blushed a deep red. She was actually *touched* by this. I didn't know Dorothy Ingram's craven heart could feel passion. I guessed we misjudged her.

I shook my head. This woman once held a gun to Mina's head. I would never, ever catch myself feeling sorry for her.

"—but as I opened the door," Wayne was saying, "I saw that the bothy was occupied."

"What?"

"Someone was living there. They weren't inside, but their stuff was strewn everywhere. There were a pile of black trousers and white shirts, all different sizes, and a pyramid of boxes from Oliver's bakery. On one wall someone had taped up a picture of your wedding announcement from the gazette and had been throwing darts at it. And weirdly, on the bed was a pile of magazines all cut up with scissors."

My blood ran cold.

Morrie looked at me. "The wait staff uniforms. The packages stolen from people's doorsteps."

"It's him," I growl. "It's the saboteur."

"It ain't no hunter," Wayne said. "Cynthia didn't want anyone hunting up there this week, not with the conference and the wedding. That's why Dorothy and I thought we wouldn't be disturbed. Whoever was there was squatting illegally, and judging by the dart sticking out of Mina's head, I thought them unhinged. I didn't want Dorothy anywhere near them, so I ran back to my car and tried to call her. Of course, the reception's poor in the woods, so I had to wait for her to show up. I grabbed her and told her we needed to leave, and we did."

I regarded Morrie. He nodded along with their story, slotting all the pieces together in his mind and comparing them with the information we had. Everything fit with what Quoth observed that day – the car we didn't recognize parked beside the bothy, the conversation he overheard where Dorothy sounded agitated. He hadn't seen Wayne there or heard his voice, but Dorothy did tend to talk over people, and Quoth had been hiding in the bushes so he didn't have a clear view of the whole place.

If Dorothy and Wayne were both at the bothy...they couldn't have murdered Iwan.

"You won't tell anyone, will you?" Dorothy said in a small voice.

"It's not our story to tell," I snapped. "But if I were you, Wayne, I would speak to your wife. She doesn't deserve this."

"And if she comes to me as a potential client looking to take revenge on her cheating husband," Morrie's whole face broke out into a devilish grin, "I'll be happy to oblige."

We left the pair of them trembling in the shed and wandered back towards the green. Morrie tapped away on his phone. We passed Grimalkin trotting off towards the church, her tail held high and quirked on the end like a periscope.

"What mischief are you up to now?" I glared at her, but she turned her nose up and sauntered past, completely ignoring us.

Morrie didn't even look up from his phone. I glared at him. "What are you doing? This is no time for playing *Crushing His Candy*."

"It's called *Candy Crush*, and I stopped playing that. It was making me crave sugar all the time, and I have to maintain my trim figure for the wedding photos. What I'm doing is texting Jo," Morrie said. "Because she has a car. Well, a WWII tank disguised as a car. We're going to go and have a look at that bothy."

Jo PULLED up outside the Rose & Wimple in her WWII tank. Morrie and I squeezed into the cab of the truck while she executed a 72-point turn in the one-way street and drove out the way she came in. Morrie insisted on sitting in the middle, long legs akimbo, stroking the gearstick lasciviously and leaving me to pack myself into the seven inches of remaining space.

"If what Morrie told me is true, then we really should call Hayes immediately," Jo said as she leaned forward to peer over the steering wheel.

"But you didn't." Morrie dug his elbow into my ribs.

"If someone's after Mina, and they've already killed once, then I feel better if we check things out first, make sure there's nothing...otherworldly."

Jo was still coming to terms with the fact that Nevermore Bookshop was magical and her best friend was the daughter of Homer and the three of us were fictional characters brought to life. She was handling it better than most people would, but then, Jo had seen some shit in her job.

Jo followed Morrie's instructions. We lurched and rattled out of the village, pulling off the lane before we reached the main driveway of Lachlan Hall onto the dirt road that led into the woods. After a mile or so, we came to the gate that Quoth had described. Morrie reached across and opened my door, forcing me to roll out. He jumped out after me, jangling a keyring in his long fingers.

"I swiped these from Wayne's shirt pocket while he was scrambling to put his boxers on," he grinned. "I knew they'd come in handy."

Morrie unlocked the gate while I leapt into the bed of the truck. I held onto the edge as Jo bumped her way along the unkempt track. The air smelled of yesterday's rain – fresh and crisp and bright. The kind of place where I felt at home.

No, not the only place. There was a chair by the fireplace in a certain bookshop, and a bright-eyed, infuriating woman snuggled under my arm, that gave me the same feeling of home.

And tomorrow, I was going to marry her.

The bothy came into view – a squat A-frame structure made of rough-sawn oak, of a type used by hunters to kip or butcher their quarry. There were no other cars here, but in the drying mud out front, I could make out tyre tracks from two vehicles. Dorothy and Wayne.

Whoever else was here had walked in.

I leapt out of the bed and circled around the back of the building. Morrie strode to the front door and unlocked it. I readied myself in case the killer tried to escape out of the open back window.

But no one appeared. Jo followed Morrie inside.

"Heathcliff, you'd better see this."

I leapt up the stairs and shoved my way inside. The bothy

was exactly as Wayne described – the pile of black-and-white uniforms thrown in a corner beside the fire, flies worshiping at the pyramid of white bakery boxes, the magazines cut up to make the sinister notes we found, the wall covered in scraps from the Argleton Gazette. Articles, photographs, and advertisements pinned around a single central image.

Mina's smiling face, with a red-tipped dart in the center of her forehead.

Rage sprang to life inside me, like a wild bear waking from winter slumber to discover his cave had been invaded. My blood quickened, the boiling sensation bubbling through my body until I no longer felt like a man in control of my person, but a beast acting on pure instinct. I gnashed my teeth. I wanted only one thing – to maim, hurt, kill this monster who wanted to hurt my Mina.

A hand fell on my shoulder. I whirled around, swinging my fist. Morrie ducked just in time to save his head from being separated from his neck.

"Save your strength, friend. The killer isn't here." Morrie nodded at the food packages. "Judging by the maggot count, I'd say they haven't been back since Dorothy and Wayne showed up and they realized they'd been discovered. They didn't even stop to remove their Mina wall."

I glared at the clippings on the wall again. They were all about Mina in some way. The criminals she helped put away, the kids read-a-thon she organized at Nevermore Bookshop, our wedding announcement. In several of the pictures, Mina's face had been scratched out with crayon.

This killer was obsessed with Mina. Who knew how long they'd been plotting this? And we were no closer to catching them.

I hate this.

I'm so *helpless.*

I opened my mouth to say something, but all that came out was a wild roar.

Jo stepped towards me. "Heathcliff, maybe—"

I threw a chair against the wall. It shattered into pieces, the crack of the splintering wood arcing through my skull. It didn't make me feel any better. I grabbed for another chair, but Jo held it out of the way.

"Destroying this place won't help me find evidence. I'm calling Hayes and Wilson," Jo said. "The two of you, go back to the village and meet all those fictional wedding guests arriving from out of town. Let me take care of this. Heathcliff, you have my promise. I'm going to SOCO the shit out of this cabin. I'll spend every spare moment I have going over every detail. The killer will have missed something. A hair, a fingernail. We'll find something that will give us an ID."

But as the three of us waited outside for the detectives and the rest of Jo's team to arrive, a stony silence settled over us. We all knew that even if Jo's team finished collecting evidence today, the SOCO examination and test results would take time we didn't have.

We were getting married tomorrow, and we had no idea who the killer was or what they had planned next.

CHAPTER 23
QUOTH

Mina and I were hanging out in Nevermore Gallery – I was hanging a new exhibition of local watercolors, and she was sitting on a stool, listening to an audiobook – when the cat door clattered. Grimalkin sauntered in, tail high in the air, looking rather pleased with herself.

"Well?" I demanded, setting down the painting of ducks beside the King's Cross stream and hitting PAUSE on the book. "Did you find Hercules?"

Grimalkin sat her ass down on the rug, facing deliberately away from us, and licked her paw.

"Grandmother," Mina said.

Lick, lick, lick.

Mina sighed. She grabbed her purse from beside her stool, pulled out a can, and slid it across the floor. "Open it yourself, Grandmother."

Grimalkin forced her shift. Her black fur retracted into her skin, her slinky legs elongating, bones cracking in new directions as her sleek cat figure transformed into an even sleeker and rather naked human.

I turned away just as she hooked a long finger through the tab on the salmon can. "This isn't the one with lemon pepper," she scolded Mina. I heard the can pop. "You know that I like the one with lemon pepper."

"Just tell us what you saw, Grimalkin."

"Humans, so impatient." Grimalkin made happy chewing sounds. "You really need to learn how to stop and smell the roses—"

"Don't make me turn on the vacuum cleaner."

"Fine, fine. Hercules is not the cat you're looking for. He said that he's been eyeing up that duck for months, but James Pond bit his tail through the mesh of the cage once when he got too close, so he decided it wasn't worth the trouble."

Mina sighed again. "What about another cat? Maybe that handsome fellow who's been hanging around—"

Grimalkin's voice was ice. "My Minnaloushe is *not* your duck-napper. I would have smelled duck on his breath, and inquired as to why he hadn't shared with me. I took the liberty of asking around the scent trails for your walking dinner, but none of the local cats are claiming the kill. Mr. Muffins said that something must be going on with the local ducks, because he used to chase a duck family that lived beside the Kings' Copse stream, but they seem to have disappeared. He said you could try talking to the ducks that live on the pond at the Lachlan estate, maybe they could tell you what's going on. Now, unless you have more manual labour you plan to subject me to, I have a hot date with this salmon."

Grimalkin made a purring noise as she slurped at the tin with her tongue. I took Mina's hand and led her into the art studio so we didn't have to watch her naked grandmother demolish her prize. As soon as I closed the studio partition behind us, Mina threw herself down on the paint-splattered sofa.

"It's no use." Mina buried her face into a cushion. "I'm out of ideas. I think James Pond is gone forever. I couldn't even find a bloody missing duck."

I knelt down beside her, my fingers trailing a pattern of swirls over her back, something that usually calms her. "Mina, what's wrong? You don't sound like yourself. It's not like you to give up."

"What choice do I have? I've ruled out my chief suspects, and Nevermore is going to be filled with our wedding guests soon. I'm out of time. I have to face it, Quoth, I thought I was good at solving mysteries, but I think I've just got lucky so far. I mean, with Angus Donahue, I didn't figure it out until he put the scarf around my neck, and with Brenda Winstone, I just *happened* to smell her husband's body in the linen cupboard... I'm useless at detective work. I'm useless at *everything*."

Her shoulders trembled, and my heart turned to lead in my chest. I knew this wasn't really about James Pond. Mina was still upset about her book launch.

The beautiful, confident woman who'd captured my soul was retreating into herself, exactly the way I used to do. I'd hide up in my attic, painting canvas after canvas while staring out the window and wishing fervently that I was someone else, someone normal, someone who didn't suffer this affliction that kept me apart.

Mina taught me that I didn't have to hide away, that I could find a place in the world where people loved and appreciated me, just as I am. I could be different without being apart. She'd been the one to encourage me to sell my artwork and sign up for art school, even as she was dealing with the fallout of her diagnosis.

My girl had worked so hard not to feel apart because of her vision, and when Jen said those things to her, and not one of her book people RSVPed, it made her feel apart again. Sometimes, we think that our scars have healed over, and then one tiny action tears them open once more, as raw and bloody as the first time we were cut.

Mina was bleeding in front of me, and this time, I knew what I had to do to help her. I knew, because it was exactly what she did to help me.

I needed to make her *see* herself again.

"I can't remember the last time you were in my studio," I said, slowly running my fingers in wide circles over her back, down her bare shoulders and arms.

"Probably before you kicked me out so you could do all your secret wedding stuff." She let out a single laugh, but there was no humor in it.

"True. But I don't have any secrets here anymore. I'm working on something new. A masterpiece. I want to show you." I slotted my finger into hers and tugged, encouraging her to sit up.

Mina knelt back on her knees, and I leaned in, running my fingertips along the back of her exposed neck. Goosebumps prickled from my touch as she shivered.

Catching her gasp on my lips, I kissed her slowly, deeply. I tried to use my body to show her how beautiful she was. How much she deserved to be worshiped. No matter what happened with her book, *she* was incredible to me.

Mina's tongue met mine in a delicious dance, and when she moaned into my mouth, I couldn't hold back my groan. My cock came to life beneath my trousers, but this wasn't about me. I had to *show* her. I had to make her see what I saw in her, what she meant to me and Heathcliff and Morrie and everyone whose life she touched with her brightness.

I grabbed the hem of her vest and tugged it over her head, exposing her pale skin and the exquisite curve of her stomach. I broke our kiss to trail my tongue along her collarbone and kiss over the curve of her breasts as I removed her bra.

As much as I wanted to take her right there, I drew back. My lips stung, begging to return to hers. And it didn't help when she looked the way she did, her eyes all inky and drunk, her hair tousled and plastered to her cheek.

"What about that artwork you were going to show me?" Her words came out breathy as she raised herself on her knees, chasing the heat of our kiss.

"She's right here." I picked her up beneath the arms and lifted her.

"Hey!" Mina yelped as I carried her over to my easel and set her feet on the floor. I knelt in front of her, my fingers undoing the buttons on her black wide-leg trousers, sending them and her knickers toppling to the floor.

Mina Wilde stood before me, beautiful in her skin, so perfect I had to bite my lip to keep from wanting to cry.

My muse. My fiancée. And today, my *canvas*.

I stepped back, adjusting myself as I rummaged through my brushes for a clean one.

"This is a Morrie-level dirty trick, leaving me here after that kiss," Mina pouted.

Once I found a clean brush and swirled it in an emerald green that reminded me of her eyes, I whirled back to her, crouching down and breathing along the bare skin of her leg, watching the goosebumps prickle.

Mina didn't say anything, but her breathing picked up as I slowly dragged the brush from her ankle up to her knee, painting everything she was to me.

"Every time I sit down to paint in this studio, I remember the first time you came to my room in the attic. The first time you truly saw me. You were so taken with my artwork that you didn't even notice me at first, sitting on the bed with a beak and black feathered wings retracting into my back."

I punctuated each word, swirling the brush down her kneecap and then up to her thigh, watching her legs tremble under my touch.

"And when you looked at me, you didn't freak out or scream or run away. Well, you did a little freak-out. But you looked as if...as if everything in your life had suddenly fallen into place. As if my strangeness somehow made me *relatable* to you. Knowable. You don't know how long I wished for that."

"Haven't you heard?" she said ruefully, her voice trembling a little as I continued my path with the brush. "I'm not *relatable*."

"You are to me."

I wiped the paint off the brush and washed it, returning to her with clean bristles. Pushing her legs apart, I traced the brush up her bare thighs, relishing in the way she shivered under my touch.

"Quoth, you forget that I've seen your paintings. Even now, the memory of your colors and lines is imprinted in my mind. You are an *objectively* incredible artist. You've spent years honing your gift, and all you needed was a little confidence to put your work out in the world." Her words wavered as I dragged the brush over her pussy, circling it around her clit. "But I'm...I'm no writer. I thought this was what I was supposed to do, the creative path that called me now that I'm done with the fashion world, but I was wrong. I'm supposed to run the bookshop and that's it. I should be happy with that."

"You're an objectively good writer, Mina. Take it from someone who is borne of literature. Everything I am is words on a page – a dream within a dream. I know of which I speak. But objectivity matters little in a creative pursuit. I know this, too. My creator toiled for his whole life for critical recognition of his work, and received it only after his death. In Poe's obituary in the New York Tribune, a critic named Rufus Griswold wrote that 'few will be grieved' by his death. I thought that was my path, too. On the path to being a working artist, you will encounter more critics than heralds. Every critique stings. Every review flays open your skin and lays your organs bare for the vultures to feed upon." I pressed the brush against her, listening to the delicious sound she made. "But if you have something to say about the world, you have to keep going despite the open wounds, because someone out there needs to hear it."

"Quoth, I..."

Her legs trembled as I moved the brush to tease her entrance, before returning to circle her clit.

"You say my work is *objectively* good. I don't see how. I never saw my work as anything special or worthwhile. But you did, Mina. Everything I've created since has been because of you. Sometimes, it takes someone else to really see the beauty in our creations. You might not see the beauty in your words, but I do. Just like my artwork, sometimes it takes someone else to really help us see it."

She shook her head. "I don't think it's really the same."

"What can I do to convince you?" I asked, slowly swirling my paintbrush over her damp panties.

She let out a shaky breath. "*Quoth.*"

"Mina."

I said her name like a prayer, leaning closer so that my words would fall between her legs.

"Do you know how beautiful you are?"

She shuddered as I kissed her mound.

"Not just your body. But your soul. The way you see people for who they really are. It's what makes you a great amateur detective, bookstore owner, writer, and an even better friend.

You make people feel welcome and loved and interesting. Being near you is like being bathed in sunlight."

She swallowed hard, and when she didn't respond, I laved my tongue over her clit and relished in her shivering thighs around me. "See? So beautiful."

Tasting her was sweeter than the wedding cake that the saboteur destroyed, but I wanted more than just to have her come on my tongue. I wanted *all* of the beautiful woman I'd fallen in love with. I wanted her to know how amazing she was and *exactly* how she deserved to be worshiped.

If my words wouldn't get her, maybe my actions would.

Mina's hands went to my head. Her fingers tangled through my hair, pulling it loose of its ribbon as I wrapped my lips over her wanting clit, sucking on the hardened nub before returning to laving it with the flat of my tongue.

Her little moans filled the air as she bucked her hips to meet my tongue. But I wasn't going to let her come yet.

I pulled my lips away, kissing a trail down her thigh before pulling back.

"Tell me that you know you're amazing. Tell me that your words have value."

"Quoth," she breathed.

"Tell me, or I'm not going to let you come," I said with a laugh, kissing the back of her knee, her calves, anywhere but where she wanted it.

Fuck, if my cock wasn't already aching, now it was straining against my trousers, begging to be buried deep inside her.

But I needed to take it slow. I needed her to understand the beauty in being an artist and being raw and vulnerable to the world.

"Quoth..."

"*Say* it."

"I'm amazing," she muttered.

"Nope, that doesn't count. I need you to say it louder. Shout it," I said, gazing up at her. Her pretty pink nipples stared back at me, and I wanted to taste them.

But I held back, gripping onto her knees.

"Say it, Mina."

"I'm amazing," she said with a laugh as she tilted her head back. "This is ridiculous."

"No." I brushed my lips over her clit again. "It's not ridiculous. Say the rest of it."

"I'm amazing! I'm amazing and my words have value!" she screamed as I sucked her clit into my mouth.

She came apart around me, her hands gripping my shoulders and her knees digging into me as she slumped forward. Her legs clamped around my head as she rode out her orgasm. I tasted her sweetness on my tongue, and I didn't want to eat or drink anything else ever again. She sated me in a way that food never could.

"See, that wasn't so hard, was it?" I asked, getting to my feet and taking her lips in mine.

I wrapped my arms around her, pulling her against me, wishing I could get closer still, that I could crawl inside her skin and push out all those bad feelings and doubts she had about herself.

Mina's kisses were desperate, pleading, as she tugged apart the buttons on my shirt, forcing me out of my clothes so she could press her naked body against mine. Our skin sizzled and burned where we touched – rows of fire ants dancing conga lines across our bodies.

Picking Mina up around the waist, I laid her down on the table, never breaking our kiss. My hands roamed over her body, my fingers dragging over her nipples until she bit down on my tongue with need.

When I couldn't take any more and I thought my body

would implode from wanting her, I pulled back and lined myself up against her entrance, the head of my cock teasing her as she thrust her hips against me, trying to drive me inside her.

"Tell me that you know you're beautiful, inside and out."

"Quoth," she said again with a laugh. "You have been hanging around Morrie too long."

"Tell me, please," I begged, my cock jerking with need of her. She angled her hips, trying to get me to give in, but I wouldn't do it. "Tell me, Mina. You're tearing me apart."

"I'm beautiful inside and out, and so are you." She let out a deep breath as I slid inside her.

She felt amazing, her warmth squeezing around me. She gripped onto my back as I thrust inside her and claimed her lips in a hungry kiss.

"You're so beautiful, Mina. Not just your eyes and your hair and your mind, but your soul," I whispered against her lips before leaving a trail of kisses on the tip of her nose, over her cheek, and down her neck.

Mina's pulse raced against mine. Her hands scrambled against the table, knocking brushes and palettes onto the floor.

Gripping onto the sides of her face, I met her heated gaze. "I mean it, Mina. You're beautiful. You deserve to be worshiped and to bare your soul for the world."

A single tear fell from her eye, and I wiped it away. "Don't cry, please. I don't want to make you cry."

She tightened around me, her chest rising with her ragged breath. "I'm not crying because I'm sad; it's because of how you make me feel. It's..." she sighed, her eyes closing slowly then opening again. "Beautiful, I guess."

"There is no exquisite beauty without some strangeness in the proportions," I said seriously. "Someone told me that once."

Mina laughed, but her breath caught in her throat as she gripped onto my waist, her hips meeting mine.

"You're so beautiful," I whispered again, thrusting hard and relishing the way her body fit so perfectly in mine.

"So. Beautiful." I punctuated my words with each thrust as little whimpers left her lips.

Mina gripped hard onto my waist as her body shook around me, my name spilling from her lips as she came apart for me. It didn't take too long for me to follow, spilling into her with a fierceness that made red dots dance in front of my eyes.

Brushes rolled off the table as I collapsed against her chest, holding her to me, never wanting to let her go. We didn't say anything for a while; we just lay together, our hearts beating together, our breath kissing each other's lips.

I studied her eyes. Mina's eyes were still a window into her soul, and right now, her soul was more at peace than it had been in a long time. Maybe I didn't wholly convince her that her work was as valuable as she was, but at least it was a start—

I remembered something. "Why don't we ask Marjorie?"

"Your art teacher?" Mina blinked, trying to follow my line of thinking. "What are we asking her about?"

"She has two pet ducks. With all the wedding plans, I'd completely forgotten about it. Maybe she could give us some insight about James Pond—"

"That's perfect." Mina's face lit up, her mind already whirring with another potential lead. "Let's go talk to her right now!"

We cleaned up the studio and ourselves, and I called an Uber while Mina brushed out her long hair and made herself 'presentable' – which is ridiculous, because Mina always looked stunning, but also because Marjorie was also blind. But I know that Mina admired Marjorie greatly – she helped Mina a lot with adaptations when she started to rapidly lose her sight.

I went downstairs to wait for the car to arrive. As I opened the door to the shop, I noticed something pinned to the door. A note.

I unfolded it, my heart stuttering as I saw the same glued letters that had been on the others:

HOW WILL YOU GET MARRIED WITHOUT A CELEBRANT YOU DESTROYED MY ONE CHANCE OF HAPPINESS. I WON'T LET YOU HAVE A HAPPILY-EVER-AFTER.

CHAPTER 24

QUOTH

"Is the car here yet?" Mina appeared behind me.

Heart pounding, I folded the letter and shoved it into my pocket. Whoever was responsible for Iwan's death and the wedding sabotage, they weren't done yet. And now that we knew Wayne and Dorothy Ingram were seeing each other, and both had alibis for Iwan's murder, we had *no clue* who they could be.

"Quoth?" Mina's mouth twisted. "Is something wrong?"

I bit my tongue until I tasted blood. I wanted to tell Mina. I didn't like that she didn't know the whole story. But I wanted to speak with Heathcliff and Morrie first, in case they'd found something at the bothy that could solve the whole case without any fanfare.

"Quoth?"

"It's nothing. I'm just excited about tomorrow." I slid my arm through hers, hoping that she couldn't sense my trembling. "The car's waiting for us at the top of the street."

I got in the front while Mina climbed in back and settled Oscar into the footwell. The driver was new to us, and he made a face about the dog, which thankfully Mina didn't see, but he knew the rules about allowing service animals and pulled away without incident, dropping us off outside the art school ten minutes later.

We wandered through the vibrant art studios. Students were frantically trying to finish their end-of-term assignments. The place reeked of paint fumes and solder, smells that immediately made me feel right at home. The radio was blaring with more depressing news about the Crixley escapee and impending climate doom.

I knocked on Marjorie's door and called out who we were, since we didn't have an appointment. She flung open the door, a huge smile spreading across her face, a hot glue gun in her hand dripping clear blobs on the floor. "Allan? Mina? I'm surprised to see you here. Aren't you getting married tomorrow? Oh no, I didn't get the date wrong, did I? Don't tell me I missed the wedding. I'm so tied up in my latest project that half the time I forget to eat."

"No, you got it right. The wedding is tomorrow." I got a different kind of flutter in my chest at the thought.

"But we may have got ourselves embroiled in another mystery," Mina said with a hint of sheepishness. "And we think you might be able to help us. Quoth said that you keep ducks as pets?"

"I do." Marjorie beamed. "Birds are incredibly intelligent, especially ducks. Some researchers think they might be as clever as dogs. I wonder if one day we might be able to have guide ducks as well as guide dogs. In the meantime, Waddles and Lily give me a lot of joy. Come in, come in. Did you want to know something about ducks?"

Marjorie ushered us inside her noisy office. The metal windchimes that she made filled every corner of the room, and they tinkled and clanged from the crisp breeze blowing in the open window. I steered Mina around Marjorie's latest creation – a large chime made from recycled aluminum cans and other rubbish hanging from a frame in the center of the room. Mondrian lifted his head from under the desk, regarded us with a stoic glance, and then went back to sleep.

We took a seat on a sofa crowded with Braille pages and boxes of rubbish. Mina described where she'd got to on the case so far, and how all her leads had turned into nothing. I watched her in awe. To everyone else, this case was silly, but Mina took James Pond's disappearance as seriously as any murder case we've ever worked on.

The note burned in my pocket.

How could someone want Mina to suffer? How could anyone wish to deny this special woman anything she wanted?

Marjorie tapped her chin. "You know, I don't think that James Pond has been duck-napped at all."

"He hasn't?"

"You said that the wire was cut all rough and crooked? If it were cut with pliers, the cuts would be smooth, right?"

"That's what Morrie said, but I figured it would depend on how skilled the person was at cutting wire. I'd probably cut it like that!" Mina laughed.

"I don't think a person cut the wire at all. James Pond is a drake. People don't usually keep a drake as a pet when they have a single duck, because although some of them are lovely, they can become aggressive and try to dominate their human, especially if they don't have females around for mating." Marjorie rubbed her hands together. I think she was enjoying being part of one of our mysteries. "I think James Pond cut *himself* out of his pen."

"He cut through wire?"

"Ducks have sharp 'teeth' inside their bill. They're not technically teeth because ducks don't produce enamel, but comb-like projections called lamellae that they use for filtering while feeding. If the wire was thin and he was determined enough, he could do it."

"Maisie said that James had never tried to escape before."

"This might be him trying to assert his dominance, but more likely, I'd say that James is looking for a girlfriend. He'll roam far and wide looking for a female to mate with. I'd check around local ponds, bird shelters, or any place where ducks might normally hang out. Duck mating can be quite violent, so you may also find areas of disturbance, dirt tossed around, trees pulled up, etc."

"Thanks, Marjorie. We'll do that." Mina stood up. "Well, we'll see you at the wedding."

"And your book launch? I've got an invite to that, too, if I'm not mistaken. I'm so proud of you, Mina. I can't wait to read your book. I hope you do an audiobook version soon. I can get Alexa to read the ebook version aloud, but it's not the same."

"Oh, actually..." Hurt flashed across Mina's face. "You must not have seen my announcement. I've decided to cancel the book launch—"

"Oh, I got the notification. But I was hoping to convince you that you've made a mistake." Marjorie's voice turned stern, reminding me of when she would scold me for not pushing the boundaries of form and color in my work. "Mina, sit down. I think we need to have a talk, artist to artist."

CHAPTER 25
MINA

Marjorie's voice meant business.

I sat.

I glanced over at Quoth, hoping to convey through my facial expressions that if he had in any way engineered this, I would eviscerate him. But my raven kept hold of my hand in his lap, his body at ease.

Marjorie pulled her chair closer to me. She smelled of hot glue and etching chemicals. In the window behind her head, one of her tactile metal mobiles made a loud *CLUNK* as the late afternoon breeze hit it.

"May I ask, why have you canceled your launch? And why are you *so* obsessed with finding James Pond? Does it have something to do with your wedding?" Her voice softened. "Or your book?"

I sucked in a breath. Marjorie heard, because she patted my knee. I squeezed Quoth's hand so hard I heard him exhale.

I squeezed my eyes shut. Here, beneath the weight of these two artists who had overcome so much to put their work out in the world, I felt so *stupid*.

"Mina, what is it?"

"It's just…" I swallowed a breath. "I invited all these famous reviewers and literary people that I know through Nevermore to my book launch, and none of them were coming. Not a single one. I sent out ARC copies to reviewers, and no one took me up on it. *No one.* And I know that all my friends would have come anyway, but that makes it *worse.* I didn't want to fail in front of everyone."

"Oh, Mina, don't you see that putting out a piece of art is never failing?"

I shook my head. "An editor, Jen Whately, told me that she might've been interested in my book, but she didn't think my blind heroine would be *relatable* to readers. It's too niche, or…"

Marjorie snorted. "And let me guess, you're now second-guessing publishing the book in the first place? You're thinking about rewriting that character as a sightie? Or maybe shredding your manuscript and crawling into a hole and never writing another word ever again?"

"Pretty much," I admitted.

Quoth squeezed my hand back. "Mina, why didn't you tell me this?"

"Because I'm embarrassed." Even talking about it now made my cheeks grow hot. "I've seen how hard you've worked to overcome your shyness to put your work out there, and here I am trying to do the same thing, and I want to bail at the eleventh hour. I'm embarrassed because these people have no reason to lie to me, and it must mean that my book is destined for failure. I know *academically* that I have to take these things on the chin if I want to be a writer, but all I feel is that I'm not good enough. Still. After all this time, after all the work I've done, my blindness still makes me not enough."

"Do you think I could have done any of those things

without you?" Quoth whispered. "That's what I was trying to tell you before, Mina. Everything I've been able to achieve with my art is because of *you*."

"Can I give you some advice, one artist to another?" Marjorie asked.

I shrugged. "Sure."

"If you want to be a creative and put your work out into the world, you have to accept that your work then stops belonging to you and instead belongs to the world, and people in the world will develop opinions on it, and lots of those opinions will be wrong and cruel and dumb. Some of them will be cruel and *correct*, and those usually hurt worse. When I applied to art schools, the director at one particular institution invited me to a meeting. I thought he was offering me a place in a prestigious programme, and I was beside myself with excitement. It turned out that he wanted to *personally* talk me out of becoming an artist. He said that the art studio was dangerous, that I was a health and safety risk, especially if I wanted to work with metal. He said that they would have to make so many changes to accommodate me that I'd bankrupt the entire program. I managed to hold it together until he dismissed me, and then I burst into tears. But I decided that I wasn't going to let people like that hold me back, and I kept applying to art schools, and eventually, I found this place. They didn't just *accept* me here, they *welcomed* me. They were excited about my work and my perspective. They asked me what they could do to make the art studio safe for me, and how they could help me achieve my artistic vision.

"Time and again, you will come up against people who don't get what you're doing or why you're doing it. You might not have come up against this much in the fashion world because you were so young and at the beginning of your journey, or maybe because you weren't emotionally invested in the pieces you created. But now, because writing is like stabbing a pen into your heart and using your own blood as ink, when you face rejection, it feels like a rejection of *you*."

The tears that had been sitting at the corners of my eyes all day finally spilt over. I nodded, then remembered that Marjorie couldn't see it. "Yes," I whispered, crushing Quoth's fingers in mine.

"The truth is, this editor might be right – publishing houses might not be interested in books like yours. The world is often happier pretending that people like you and I don't exist. But we do, and there will be people out there who need your stories. Those are the people who should come to your book launch. Don't waste a single sausage roll on people who don't believe in you. Instead, go to your audience directly."

I heard her tapping away on her Perkins. Marjorie pulled out a piece of Braille paper and handed it to me.

"If you change your mind about the book launch in the future, I'm giving you the numbers of a couple of my friends. Give them a call. They'll help you get the word out amongst our community. People *will* be interested in your story, Mina. You're a bright girl with incredible creative vision. I'd hate to see you give up on this dream."

"Marjorie, I—" I couldn't say anything more because my tears were falling on the paper.

"What do you say?" Quoth squeezed my hand. "Would you consider giving the book launch another shot?"

"Maybe," I sniffed. "Yes, I think so. It's too close to the wedding to make it happen now, but I'd like to arrange it in a few weeks." I turned to Marjorie. "Will you come if the launch is back on? I might need someone to hold my hair back when I throw up."

"I wouldn't miss it," she said, her voice bright.

"Then we'll save you as many sausage rolls as you can eat," I promised.

"That's what I wanted to hear." She gave my knee a final squeeze. "Now, stop worrying about James Pond and your book, and go get married!"

MESSAGE SENT TO BOOK LAUNCH GUEST LIST FROM NEVERMORE BOOKSHOP EMAIL

URGENT: MINA'S BOOK LAUNCH IS BACK ON! AND IT'S A SURPRISE!

We might not have catering, or even copies of the book to buy, but if you show up at Nevermore Bookshop the evening after the wedding, Mina will read an excerpt from her book, take questions, and spin an incredible DJ set.

See you there!

Don't tell Mina, because it's a surprise.

And see you tomorrow at the wedding!

CHAPTER 26

MINA

Three men slept peacefully. Heathcliff's arms wrapped around me, holding me against his chest, his breath warm against my neck. On the other side of him, Morrie snored, his arm draped protectively across both of us. Quoth perched on top of the metal wall sculpture hanging over the bed, occasionally letting out a little croak as he dreamed his bird dreams.

Even though I was bone-tired, I couldn't sleep.

As soon as we finished with Marjorie, Quoth rushed off to see about some last-minute secret wedding stuff. I didn't have time to resent that, because I was in full-on wedding mode. I'd packed up my dress and makeup so Heathcliff could transport them to the Lachlan Hall bridal suite. I had a nail appointment (red glitter. If I hold them really close to my face in the right light, I can see the sparkles), and I'd been practising my dance moves and welcoming our out-of-town guests. The entire downstairs of Nevermore Bookshop was a sea of mattresses and cots to sleep our friends who'd come in from all over just for our big day.

Every time I closed my eyes, I remembered that tomorrow

I'd be walking down the aisle to a cello version of Metallica's 'Nothing Else Matters,' on my way to marry three men who I trusted would always have my back.

Men who took up *way* too much space in the bed with their heavy arms and their breathing right in my ear.

Sigh.

Nope, sleep definitely wasn't happening. Might as well get a drink and read a little beside the dwindling fire.

After a bit of wrangling, I managed to drag myself out from beneath Heathcliff and Morrie. I grabbed my phone from the charger on the dresser and shuffled toward the bathroom. One great thing about going blind is that you stop needing to turn lights on in the middle of the night.

I did my business and washed my hands, noting with a giddy feeling in my chest that Morrie's expensive bath products were gone from the sink. He'd moved them up to Lachlan Hall, where we'd get ready tomorrow.

I stepped out of the bathroom. My foot scuffed something on the floor. It crinkled like a piece of paper.

Quoth must have dropped a page from his sketchbook again. He's always doing that.

I bent down to pick it up, and my fingers brushed over familiar, thick, ancient paper, and a wax seal.

A letter.

A letter that had fallen on the carpet *directly* outside the time-travelling room.

It could only be from one person.

I raced back to the bedroom and flicked on the light. "Wake up!" I yelled.

Quoth shook out his wings, sending feathers flying. "Croooak?"

"Who's there?" Heathcliff grabbed for the long sword he kept in the corner of the room, nearly squashing Morrie in the process. "If you're the saboteur come to hurt Mina, you have to get through me first."

"The saboteur?" I asked.

He rubbed his eyes. "Just...a bad dream. Ignore me. Why are you awake? Is something wrong?"

"Everything's okay." I held up the envelope. "At least, I think it is. My father sent a letter. I thought we could read it together."

Heathcliff took the letter from me. The three of them curled around me, and Oscar jumped up and settled on my lap. Heathcliff broke the wax seal and began to read.

Beloved Mina,

I know that you didn't expect to hear from me again, but a father cannot ignore his daughter on her wedding day.

I want you to know that I am so proud of you. You are everything I could have ever wished for in a daughter – brave and wise and kind and loyal. It has been an honor to be your father from afar, and to feel the ripples of your legacy throughout time and space.

You are special, Mina Wilde. May all your dreams come true.

I have got you a wedding present. I know that you can't afford a honeymoon, but if you and your husbands open this door at precisely 10:17AM on the morning of the 22nd, you'll have an experience you'll never forget.

Love, Dad.

"Dad got us a honeymoon? We're going, right?" I grabbed for the letter, wanting to touch this object that my father had touched, wanting to deepen my connection to him.

"Do you not recall the calamities that have befallen us when last we used that room?" Heathcliff folded his arms.

"A little calamity never hurt anyone," Morrie said. "I hope it takes us to a beach on a tropical island, with trees filled with magical alcoholic coconuts."

"We couldn't afford a honeymoon otherwise," Quoth said. "I say that we should go."

"Or an opulent hotel room with 400-thread-count Egyptian cotton sheets." Morrie rubbed his fingers together. "Or on board the Orient Express right in the middle of a perplexing murder—"

"We're unlikely to end up on a train, or a beach," I reminded him, "since the room will only take us to the shop during different periods in history. But still, I think it could be fun."

"If we all get eaten by dinosaurs, I'm blaming you." Heathcliff slid back into bed.

"Fair."

"And I'm taking my sword." Heathcliff pulled me against his chest, tucking the blankets around us. "We don't know what we might find on the other side."

He kissed the top of my head. I reached out and hit my phone, which read out the time. 3:15AM. "Hey, we're getting married today! It's our wedding day!"

"I know, which is why we're going to enjoy the peace and quiet while we still have it." Heathcliff nuzzled my neck. "I spent far too long today breaking up arguments between Sherlock and David Winter. And Lydia's arriving on the early train, may the Old Gods preserve us. So why don't you close those pretty eyes of yours and try to get some sleep?"

"Only if you tell me what you meant before, about a saboteur?"

"Oh, that. Like I said, it was a bad dream." He pressed me deeper into his chest. "Go to sleep, woman. Don't try and wriggle out of this now. Later today, you are going to be my wife."

CHAPTER 27

HEATHCLIFF

I bolted upright, my mind a blur of nightmares of bloody sculptures and maggot-infested boxes and cut-out letters from the newspaper. Morrie lay curled against my chest, a pillow crease across his perfect cheekbone and an adorable line of drool hanging from the corner of his mouth.

Where's Mina? I fisted the sheets, trying to drag myself back to reality.

The clock on the bedside table read 5:45AM.

The wedding. The *wedding*.

We were getting married to Mina today.

And we still hadn't caught the killer or even figured out who they were or why they were after Mina.

A lump at my back stirred. "Why are you awake? The sun isn't even in the sky yet—" Morrie bolted upright, his eyes wide. "We're getting married today."

"Yes," I growled.

Morrie leapt to his feet, throwing the blankets off all of us. "Didn't you hear me? We're getting *married*. What are you doing lying around? We have lots to do and no time to do it. I hope you paid the water bill this month because I plan on showering for at least ninety-seven minutes. I want to look perfect for my bride—"

"We didn't catch the killer," I whispered, not sure where Mina was.

Morrie's icicle eyes narrowed. "No, but they're hardly going to be able to get away with anything in a room full of people, are they? You've got all that extra security, and in case you've forgotten, *we'll* be there. We won't let anything bad happen to her."

He was right. If only I could get rid of this niggling worry stabbing into my chest. Usually, whisky would do the trick, but today I needed to be sober. I wanted to have a clear head if the killer showed their face and...

...and I wanted to be utterly in the moment when I kissed my *bride*.

I went out to the kitchen to start the coffee machine and found Quoth already there, three steaming cups of pitch-black perfection already lined up along the kitchen counter. I gulped back all three. Quoth arched an eyebrow, but he didn't say a thing. Instead, he set a fourth cup down in front of me and stirred his herbal tea.

"Where's Mina?"

"Jo already came to pick her up. They have hair appointments."

"Before the sun is fully awake?"

"Apparently, Mina has something extravagant planned." The orange around Quoth's eyes had all but disappeared. "Do you think that we should call off the—"

"No."

"But what if the killer tries—"

"They won't."

I wish I felt as confident as I sounded. Hayes and Wilson had promised a police presence. Plus, our friend Jo had roped in the ladies from her film club as a sort of unofficial security team, and there was nothing more terrifying to a would-be murderer than an army of pissed-off lesbians.

Speaking of Jo...I checked my phone. The little message icon had a 171 next to it. That was one more text since yesterday. I pulled up her number and hit connect.

She answered with a huff. "I sent you a text. Don't you ever answer your texts?"

"No," I growled. "You're lucky you're getting a phone call. My preferred method of communication is nothing at all, followed by strongly worded letters."

"Noted. I'm pleased with the special treatment. I was just reporting that our girl is safe and sound here at Lachlan Hall. Two officers are patrolling the estate. Mina hasn't noticed them. As far as she knows, everything is fine. We're just finishing breakfast, and then the primping will commence. You don't have to worry, Heathcliff. Everything will be okay. We're not going to let this bastard ruin your day. Try to relax and focus on the fact that you're getting married—"

BANG. THUMP. CRASH.

I winced. "Got to go. See you later."

"See you—"

I tossed the phone on top of the pile of stuff I needed to bring to Lachlan Hall, grabbed my sword, and stormed downstairs, Morrie hot on my heels.

"Oooh, hey!" Victor Frankenstein shook his fist at me as I stomped over his cot. "You stood on my hand. I need those fingers for...things!"

All around the first floor, people stirred from makeshift beds. Socrates was folding his chiton while dissecting the idea of moral absolution into his phone camera for his millions of adoring fans. The headless horseman sat glumly in the corner, nodding his stump patiently as Lancelot explained his philosophy for the care and keeping of noble steeds.

I followed the sounds of an escalating argument into the customer bathroom and found David Winter – Jane Austen scholar, numismatics devotee, and fine swordsmith, wrestling a toothbrush off Sherlock and holding it triumphantly over the toilet bowl.

"What's going on?" I growled, waving my sword in their faces.

"He stole my toothbrush!" Sherlock shouted.

"Stop crowding me while I'm in the bathroom." David pinched the end, swinging the brush over the loo. "This is my toothbrush, but luckily, I have a spare. Do you?"

"Don't you *dare*. That's *my* toothbrush. I distinctly remember it because I purchase the same Star Trek toothbrush—"

"I can't believe we were ever an item." Morrie rolled his eyes as he disappeared back upstairs. He returned a moment later with a brand new, expensive-looking toothbrush still in its wrapping. He tossed it at Sherlock. "There. I won't have you breathing all over my new wife. Now, will the two of you stop bickering?"

"Much obliged." Sherlock raked a hand through his unkempt hair. "Give me twelve-and-a-half minutes to complete my toilette, and then I shall be ready to depart. And Morrie?"

Morrie raised an eyebrow.

My fingers closed around the hilt of my sword.

"You look good." Sherlock gave him a half smile that I didn't think was entirely innocent. "I mean, you look happy."

"I do, don't I?" Morrie grinned. "Better hurry, you've only got eight minutes and seventeen seconds left. The rest of you —" He glared at our guests. "We'll see you up at the hall when you're ready. Socrates is in charge of calling an Uber, and don't forget to lock up before you leave."

Morrie and Quoth called Ubers while I brought down our bags. Socrates kept tripping over the hem of his sheet, and David and Sherlock got into another argument about who had the widest cummerbund.

"Do they remind you of anyone?" Morrie asked as we climbed into our own vehicle, thankfully empty of any guests.

"They remind me of people I wish I didn't have to see again."

"They're *us*, you fool." His blue eyes sparkled. "I wouldn't be surprised if we find them snogging on the dance floor tonight."

"Spare me."

I barely paid attention to the drive. I stared at my hands and tried in vain to untangle the knots in my stomach.

You're just nervous because you want this to be perfect for Mina.

A uniformed officer stopped our car as we pulled into Lachlan Hall. I knew the police presence was meant to reassure us, but it set my teeth on edge. I hadn't exactly had the best relationship with the local constabulary, not with the whole 'keeping me in jail for the night while they proved I didn't know how to text' thing.

The wheels crunched on gravel as we pulled into the parking area. Several guest and staff cars were already here. My chest tightened as I saw Cynthia running towards us.

"What's wrong now?" I growled as I slammed the car door, narrowly missing Morrie's face.

"Nothing. Everything is fine." Her voice trembled.

"*Cynthia.*"

"It's nothing. We've had a bit of trouble with the decorations, and I think someone might have been poaching on our property. All the birds have disappeared from the pond." She must've seen my face because she brightened. "But we're fixing it! Don't worry. This wedding is going to go perfectly. The staff are offering your guests food and cocktails in the Yellow Drawing Room. I'll show the three of you to your suite."

Cynthia led us up the opulent staircase and through the winding corridors to a suite of rooms overlooking the now-empty pond. "You'll sleep in the bridal suite this evening," she said. "That's just down the hall. But I've set this room aside for you to get ready. All of Morrie's toiletries are set up in the rain shower. Your suits were pressed this morning and are hanging by the window, and I'll have some snacks and bubbles sent up—"

"What happened to the decorations?" I growled.

"Nothing, nothing." Her face clouded over. "Well, we went to put out the Beauty and the Beast characters this morning, and a few of them appear to have been...stabbed."

"Stabbed?" Quoth's face fell.

"Not to worry, I have my staff in there right now, doing some emergency repairs. If you don't need anything else, I must run. I've got a wedding to pull off!"

Cynthia practically leapt for the door, slamming it shut behind her.

Quoth slumped in the armchair, his hair falling over his face. "What are we going to do?"

Morrie patted his shoulder. "I'm sure the decorations will look fine—"

"I don't care about the decorations! I care that this killer is somewhere on the property. They've already gotten close enough to ruin the decorations. Mina is right *here*." His eyes flashed at me. "And she doesn't even know that she's in danger."

I flopped down on the opposite chair, my head falling into my hands. "Do you want me to admit that you're right? Fine. You're right, birdie. We should have told her. I didn't want her to feel afraid on her wedding day, but she should have at least known what she was walking into. If you want me to, I'll storm into the bridal suite now and tell her."

"What are we going to do?" Quoth's eyes brimmed with tears.

"We're here now," Morrie said brightly as he checked his cologne. "I've just texted Hayes to let him know what happened, and he says that he's sending extra people. I've told Jo to be extra vigilant, too, and Lydia's in there with Mina and Jo now. The killer may be sneaky, but no way will they be able to endure Lydia to get to our girl. She's as protected as she can be. We don't gain anything by busting in there and telling her."

"Except that we'd get to see her." Quoth stood and grabbed his suit from the rack. He started stripping off his clothes like he was the world's angriest chicken. "We'd know she's okay."

"Exactly. We'd see her. It's bad luck to see the bride before the wedding. We don't need any more bad luck. There is absolutely nothing else that can go wrong with this wedding now."

"I wouldn't speak too soon." Quoth made a face as he pulled our waistcoats out of the garment bag.

My jaw fell open.

How is that even possible?

All three waistcoats had an enormous hole gnawed through them. It looked as though something had eaten its way through one side of the fabric and out the other side.

"I...I don't understand." Morrie's blue eyes drained of verve. "How did—"

"That's it." I yanked my suit off the rank and tossed it in the bin. "I give up. I just want to see Mina."

"Wait. I think I can solve this." Quoth rummaged around in the dresser drawers, croaking with triumph as he pulled out a sewing kit. He took a pair of scissors and started cutting into his waistcoat.

Morrie and I watched, jaws on the floor, as bits of expensive silk flew everywhere.

"Ta-da!" Quoth grinned as he held up his creation. He'd cut out a waistcoat shape from the back panel.

Morrie looked like he was trying not to laugh. "I don't know what school of tailoring you went to, birdie, but that's only half a waistcoat."

"Right." Quoth nodded. "A front half. The *important* half. What we do is glue these waistcoats to our shirts and put our jackets over the top. As long as we don't take off our jackets, no one will know that our waistcoats don't have backs."

"So, we're going to get married with cut-out waistcoats glued to our shirts?" Morrie looked aghast.

"Of course we bloody are." I fished out my shirt. "We're getting down that aisle to our Mina, no matter what."

Morrie bent down and kissed Quoth full on the lips. "You, birdie, are a genius."

"I know. Let's hurry before anything else goes wrong. Heathcliff, get in the shower. You know Morrie's going to take forever."

After a vigorous wash, I pulled my shirt over my head and held out my arms while Quoth pinned and glued. I winced as hot glue scalded my skin, but Mina was worth any level of pain. When he finished, I shrugged on my jacket and ran gelled fingers through my unruly hair.

"You look exactly how she'd want you to look." Morrie kissed the top of my head as he emerged from a steamy bathroom, wrapped in towels like Egypt's hottest mummy. "You look like you're ready to burn the world for her and you'll look damn fine doing it."

"Good."

Once he'd finished primping and preening, and Quoth had glued on his waistcoat, Morrie linked his arm in mine. After a moment of hesitation, Quoth slipped his hand through my other arm and the three of us left our room and descended the stairs.

"We should check in with Jo," Morrie said. "I want to know that Mina's—"

"There she is!" I pointed over the balustrade, where Mina stood like an enormous white meringue, waving her arms at her mother, who had a box of monogrammed plastic coffee cups and looked terrifyingly pleased with herself.

"We should take the other staircase." Morrie dragged me back. "It's bad luck to—"

"Mina!"

My heart shattered to pieces, and my vision swirled with blood, as my beloved Mina collapsed on the floor.

CHAPTER 28

MINA

"Mum, that's very thoughtful, but I don't know if we have time to set out these *very attractive* coffee cups at each place setting—"

They *were* not very attractive. According to Jo and Bree, they were a lurid green colour, and the monogrammed H on them was all wonky. But I was in survival mode and the photographer wanted me in the garden five minutes ago for some portraits with Jo and Bree and Lydia, and I was still stressing about what Heathcliff had yelled this morning about the 'saboteur'—

"Oh, honey, don't you worry about a thing. I'll just pop into the dining room while you do your photos and set them up myself. I already have to go back there, because I see that Cynthia's forgotten to lay out my napkins. I showed her that if you fold them lengthways, no one can see the burn marks—"

"Arf Arf!"

Oscar was being such a good boy today, but the whole house was a hive of stimulation, and the wait staff flowing past us carrying tiny cocktail meatballs to the early guests was just one distraction too many. He pulled on his lead, which normally wouldn't be a problem, except that I was wearing seventeen layers of silk and tulle, and I tripped on the dress, fell across his harness, and sprawled out unglamourously across the foyer floor.

Ow. Owie.

"Mina, honey, are you okay—argh!"

I turned toward Mum, but before I could get to my feet, something hit me with the force of a freight train, sending me skidding on my skirts across the foyer. The air fled my lungs.

I gasped for breath, clutching my stomach as the heavy weight untangled itself from my ample skirts and tried to pick me up.

"Mina, Mina." Heathcliff's voice was wild. "Are you hurt? Are you okay? Where is he? Where's the fiend hiding?"

I rubbed my throbbing arse. "I'm fine, apart from some crazy groom bowling me over. What are you doing?"

"You're okay?" He brushed his hands over me. "He didn't hurt you?"

"No one hurt me. I tripped. Floor-length dresses and guide-dog harnesses don't exactly go together. Why are you here? It's bad luck to see the bride before the wedding."

"I saw you go down. I thought..." His voice trailed off as Morrie and Quoth came up behind him. Quoth made a desperate sound and Morrie didn't make a single wisecrack, which made me instantly suspicious.

"What?" I snapped. "What did you think?"

The guilty, miserable look on his face broke something inside me. *This is what he's been hiding from me.* "What's going on? The three of you have been acting strangely for the last few days. You're keeping secrets, and not just about the wedding plans."

"Someone is trying to sabotage the wedding!" Quoth cried out. "I wanted to tell you, but these two talked me out of it."

"You were so stressed about your book launch, we didn't want you to worry," Morrie said.

"We thought we could catch them," Heathcliff growled.

"Wait, what do you mean, sabotaging the wedding?"

"They destroyed the wedding cake, cut the chair covers into slivers, stabbed the decorations Quoth made, left threatening notes about you, and..."

"They killed Iwan, didn't they?" I staggered back, my stomach dropping into my boots. *This can't be true, can it?*

But the silence that greeted me confirmed my fear.

"This person killed our celebrant and you didn't even *tell* me? All our friends and family are here today, everyone we care about, and you put them all in danger."

"Hayes has officers surrounding the property, and undercover cops in the crowd. He and Wilson are here, don't forget. You're the one who forced me to invite them. They're checking all the guests at the gate. Jo's got her crew of lesbian film critics watching as well, and Lydia and her soldiers are ready to jump into the fray." Heathcliff growled. "We promise, this scoundrel is not going to ruin our special day."

"Maybe not, but we shouldn't have taken the chance. I can't believe you didn't trust me with this."

Someone reached for my hand, but I shoved them away. How could they? After everything we'd been through together, after all the murders I'd solved and scrapes I'd got us out of, they didn't think I could handle this.

They don't think I'm capable.

"Mina, what do you want to do?" Quoth's voice trembled. "If you don't want to marry us, we understand."

"No, we bloody do *not* understand," Heathcliff shot back at him. "Mina is ours and we are hers and no sodding saboteur is going to stop us from making her our wife."

But I kept coming back to those words in Jen's letter, how

much they'd cut me, and how Heathcliff and Morrie and Quoth had swooped in to reassure me that she didn't know what she was talking about. But did they really believe that? Or did they think that now that I couldn't see, that I had to be protected from bad things, instead of helping them work together to solve them?

Was I *less than* in my own marriage?

"Mina?" Quoth's voice croaked.

No, don't be silly. You're only thinking that because you're still nervous about the book launch. This is Heathcliff, Morrie, and Quoth. You have come so far and been through so much together. You want to marry them. You all deserve this day.

I remembered when I first met Iwan, and he was telling me about his early days campaigning for same-sex marriage, people told him that it would never happen in this country. They'd been so certain that things couldn't change, and then they did. I thought about everything Marjorie had said, about not giving up a single sausage roll to people who don't believe in you.

Whoever this horrible saboteur was, I couldn't let them ruin this special day. I held out a shaking hand to the guys, and one by one, they placed their palms on top of mine.

"Let's do this," I beamed. "Let's get married."

"ARE YOU READY FOR THIS?" Bree asked as she and Jo lined up with me and Oscar outside the doors to the ballroom. All our guests were inside and the cello quartet were valiantly attempting a cover of my favorite Misfits song that would've been *hilarious* if my stomach weren't churning with nerves.

"Ready as I'll ever be. Wait, have you looked around?" I grabbed Jo's arm as she swung the door open a crack. "Can you see anyone who isn't supposed to be here? Do you know anything about the bothy? What did you find out from Iwan's autopsy?"

"Mina, please, don't worry about it. My team at the lab are all over the bothy evidence. We'll get results in the next day or so. And you're surrounded by people here to protect you. For once, let your friends and the police look out for you, and just enjoy your special day."

"But—"

"But nothing." Jo pressed her finger over my lips. "Zip it. That's your music starting. Let's go."

Let's go? There could be a killer out there, and she's saying let's go?

Jo gave me a gentle nudge through the door, and I forced my feet to move and my hands to give Oscar his signals.

Jo and Bree set off down the aisle, and the music swelled and everyone stood up as I took my first steps. The dress felt like it weighed a million tonnes. My hands trembled. I struggled to keep my grip on Oscar's ribbon-adorned harness.

This was supposed to be the happiest day of my life, but I couldn't stop thinking about poor Iwan.

He *died* because this saboteur didn't think that I deserved to get married.

Everyone in the world who I cared about was in this room, right now, oohing and aahing and dabbing their eyes with handkerchiefs monogrammed with crooked H's.

What if the killer tries to hurt them?

Stop it. Morrie's right. No killer would be dumb enough to try something with so many people around. Hayes has men stationed all around the wedding. He won't let anything bad happen.

But I didn't *feel* safe. I felt utterly lost and alone. The guys kept me in the dark about this. I could have helped them look for clues. Like in the notes. I hadn't even seen the notes the killer left, and maybe they gave themselves away but the guys didn't notice…

They didn't think I could handle it. They thought I had to be protected from the truth, instead of helping them solve this mystery together.

They *did* think I was different because I'd lost my eyesight.

Less than.

I'm not ready to marry them.

The thought hit me like a smack in the face. I stumbled over my dress but managed to right myself before I fell over.

The music reached a crescendo, screaming in my head.

I'm not ready to marry them.

If Heathcliff, Morrie, and Quoth didn't believe in me enough to trust me, then everything I thought we had was a lie. I needed to talk to them, alone, and figure this out. Otherwise, every word that we speak in our vows will be a lie.

But what could I do? I was literally *walking down the aisle.* I could hear my mother crying loudly, other people blowing their noses, murmuring about how pretty my dress looked. The corset was so tight that I couldn't breathe.

Impeccable timing, as always, Mina.

Tears pooled beneath my eyes, but they weren't tears of happiness. I gripped Oscar's harness so hard that my hand started to cramp.

What am I going to do?

We reached the archway, lit on both sides by tall candelabras filled with glittering candles. The whole room looked amazing, filled with flickering candlelight and strategically-placed lamps that delighted my eyes and meant I could see the outlines of the space.

It's perfect. Heathcliff did all this for me.

But right now, that didn't matter. What mattered was that Heathcliff didn't trust in me enough to tell me when a killer was after me. We should have figured this out together, the way we always did. But they left me out of it, and the killer was still out there…

"Mina," Heathcliff came down from the riser, looping his hand on mine. His lips brushed my forehead through my veil, but instead of feeling my usual zing of love, all I wanted to do was run.

Heathcliff started pulling me up the steps.

"Wait," I whimpered. "Stop, please."

"Stop?" He sounded confused. "What's wrong?"

"I don't think I want to do this," I whispered, aware of hundreds of pairs of eyes on us. "Not after what you told me today. Someone was threatening me and you didn't even think I deserved to know. That's not how you start a marriage of equals."

"Mina," Heathcliff's voice cracked. "I never intended to hurt you or to make you feel lacking. I wanted to protect you—"

"I'm not some simpering heroine in a gothic romance who needs protecting!" I hissed, the anger and hurt rising inside me. "I thought that we were partners. But I guess that was all just crap. When it comes down to it, you three see me just like all those reviewers see me, as someone to be pitied."

Oof. I'd raised my voice louder than I realized. The guests murmured to each other, shifting in their chairs. My mother hissed something at the band, who started playing at a raised volume to cover our argument.

"What can we do?" Quoth asked. He and Morrie moved around me, surrounding me. "How can we show you that we don't pity you? Mina, you're our whole world. Please—"

His words were cut off by a loud *CRASH*.

Guests screamed. The main lights in the room flickered out. I whirled around, my heart in my throat.

One of the sculptures must have fallen down, but how—

"Iwan's killer is here!" someone yelled.

"Don't be ridiculous. The statue cut the lighting cable," Cynthia cried. "My team will fix it. Hold on—"

SMASH.

"Everyone remain calm," Hayes' voice cut over the chaos. "The killer isn't here. It's just that infernal—"

"QUACK!"

What?

"QUACK QUACK QUACK!"

Before I had the chance to orient myself, a row of black and white ducks ran from beneath the carnage by the door, heading down the aisle directly for me. And they were followed by a loud, yellow—

"James Pond!"

He's here. We found him!

It all made sense now. He got out of his cage and went in search of a girlfriend. After he discovered that he couldn't find the ducks down by the Kings Copse stream, he must have come to Lachlan Hall to chat up the ducks on Cynthia's pond, none of whom sounded keen to be his girlfriend. They hopped up on the dais and scattered in all directions, while—

"James, no!" Maisie rushed after him. She dove for the duck, but he flapped his wings and scooted under her arms, knocking over the candelabra on my left.

In slow motion, the candlelight flickered as the stand toppled over...

...onto my dress.

I yelled and leapt back, but the fall must have snuffed out the candles because I couldn't feel any heat. My beautiful dress was safe at least—

"Um, gorgeous..." Morrie's face collapsed as he suddenly bent to his knees and started tugging on my skirts. For a single, terrifying moment, I thought that he was going to calm me down in typical Morrie fashion, by crawling underneath my dress and using his tongue to make me scream in front of everyone.

But *then* I smelled the burning.

Panic flared in my chest, but I couldn't do anything. As people screamed and scattered about the room, Morrie used his suit jacket to smother the flames. As he stood up, I noticed that he only had a waistcoat on his front side. His back was just a shirt. *What?*

"You're okay, gorgeous," he breathed, tossing his jacket away as he slid his arms around me.

I reached down and felt for the hem of my dress. Only, it wasn't there anymore. My hands found a singed edge.

My beautiful dress. It was completely ruined.

And not only my dress…all around me, guests ran about, hid under chairs, or fled into the drawing room and slipped on ruined food as the ducks ran wild through the chaos, tearing at the decorations and knocking people down in their attempts to escape horny James Pond.

"James, no, stay out of the catering. James, get away from there! That food isn't for ducks—"

CRASH.

"QUACK QUACK QUACK QUACK!"

Heathcliff grabbed the drake by his neck and hoisted him off the ground. "You've caused just about enough carnage here," he growled. "I was hoping there'd be duck on the dinner menu."

"QUACK!" James beat at Heathcliff's face with his wings.

"No, please! He didn't mean to." Maisie ran over, tugging on Heathcliff's arm. "Please, he's my baby."

"Mina?" Heathcliff turned to me, his voice wavering.

"Let him go," I whispered. "We're not punishing James for being who he is."

"Give us fifteen minutes to straighten everything out," Morrie said, his voice bursting with confidence. "And we'll be back to the wedding."

"No."

The moment the word left my mouth, I felt the truth behind it.

Our wedding was cursed.

And I wasn't ready.

"Mina, wait!"

But I didn't wait. I had to get out of there.

I turned on my heel, gripped Oscar's harness, and, wiping away the tears, gave him his instructions. "Oscar, take me away from here."

CHAPTER 29

MINA

The room fell eerily silent as Oscar picked his way through the broken sculptures and upturned chairs towards the main ballroom doors. Not even my mother came after me, a fact for which I would be eternally grateful.

I needed space. I needed to *think*.

Oscar found his way back through the labyrinth of Lachlan Hall's rooms to the grand entrance hall. I stepped outside. A crisp breeze raised goose pimples on my bare shoulders, and the veil stuck to my tear-stained cheeks as I descended the marble steps.

A pair of limo drivers were leaning against the hood of a limo, sharing a smoke. They sprung apart as Oscar and I approached.

"Are you all done in there, ma'am? We're here to take you to the photography location. Only..." I could feel his gaze sweeping over me. "Where are your husbands? And the bridesmaids? And the mother of the bride?"

"Why does your dress smell singed?" asked the other – a woman, her voice croaky from the cigarette.

"No one else is coming. It's just me." I swiped my hand across my cheeks, only managing to make my veil even stickier. "Take me into the village. Please."

Neither of them moved.

I thrust my hand on my hip. "Are you really going to deny a bride on her wedding day?"

"Arf," Oscar added.

"When you put it like that." The woman leapt up and opened the door for me. "Hop on in, ma'am."

I balled my ruined dress in my arms and half climbed, half flopped into the limo. I settled Oscar at my feet and collapsed into the long leather couch. A bottle of Champagne sat in an ice bucket, along with a rack of glasses and a little fridge filled with cans of fancy gin and tonic. I grabbed a can and cracked it, and shoved two more into my cleavage.

The only thing that had been keeping me sane since the turmoil with my book was knowing that everything in my relationship was perfect. That even if the world saw me as someone different, less than, 'not relatable,' to Heathcliff, Morrie, and Quoth, I was exactly the same Mina that I'd always been.

But that wasn't true, was it?

How could I marry them now?

I raised the glass to my lips, fighting with my veil so I could take a long drink. I thought I heard a faint 'quack' from the other end of the limo, but obviously, I was just imagining it.

"We've arrived at the village green, ma'am," the driver called. "Did you want me to wait for you, or—"

"No." I flung myself out of the door, untangled Oscar's lead from around my legs, and took off across the green.

I didn't even look where I was going as I ran through the village, my white bridal Docs skidding over the ancient cobbles. My eyes blurred with tears. All I knew was that I needed to get away.

This is all my fault.

I'd tried to have it all. I tried to tell myself that I was the same person as I'd always been. I let down everyone, and I put everyone I love in danger. And now I was running from my own wedding.

I couldn't go back to Nevermore Bookshop. I couldn't sit in that empty building surrounded by all the memories of them, of the place where I found myself again, and think about this *rationally*. I needed to figure out what my heart was doing, what this crushing sensation in my chest meant.

My heart pounded against my ribs, and pain shot from my empty stomach down my leg. I stopped, my hands on my knees as I fought to catch my breath.

When I looked up, I saw that I was in front of Argleton Presbyterian Church.

And suddenly, despite all the trouble religious people had caused me, that open door looked like the most inviting place in the world.

I stepped inside. My boots squeaked on the polished floor.

"Hello?" I called out, but there was no reply.

My feet led me across the nave to the spiral staircase leading to the bell tower. A flash of memory caught me unaware. Nearly a year ago, I found a pregnant Ginny Button at the bottom of these same steps, her neck snapped after she was pushed. I stepped over the spot where her body was found. My fingers trembled as I fumbled for the velvet rope blocking off the staircase, and climbed over.

Oscar whimpered as I directed him up the staircase, pushing back against my command. It wasn't like him to disobey unless there was a danger I couldn't see, but there wasn't any danger on the staircase apart from slipping on the ancient steps. He'd had a lot of stimulation today. After another try, he moved forward, and we started to climb. My boots slipped and slid over the worn, uneven stone steps. I kept one hand tight on Oscar's harness and the other on the wall to steady myself in the narrow curving staircase.

By now, the guys would be looking all over the village for me. Heathcliff would be tearing his hair out with rage.

It wasn't his fault, any of this. It was my fault for thinking that everything would be the same. But I had to sort out my heart before I could speak to them. I just needed a few moments to gather myself.

My chest heaved as I made it to the top of the stairs. Oscar panted from the climb. My hands felt around the edges of the heavy wooden door until they located the handle. I pushed outward, relieved when the door gave way and I was greeted by a blast of cool air.

I clambered out onto the roof of the bell tower. It was a small square space with a narrow stone walkway around the edge, and a glass and lead peaked roof in the center. Up here, the wind tore through the village, pelting me from three directions and plastering my veil to my face.

I tore it out of my hair and tossed it over the edge. Whoever thought veils were a good idea?

I leaned against the railing and removed one of the G&Ts from my bra. I cracked it open. Drinking helped with the thinking. Oscar pawed at my leg.

"Oscar, sit."

Once again, he wasn't listening to me. He made the whining noise that I'd come to recognise as his signal for danger.

"Oscar, I know this has been a rough day, and you're overstimulated, but I need you to remember your training. I need to think—"

"Hello, Mina."

The voice, familiar for all the wrong reasons, turned my blood to ice.

I'm not alone on this roof.

CHAPTER 30

MINA

The voice sent a shockwave through my body. *I never thought I'd hear it again.*

"Mrs. Winstone?"

"You remember me. I'm so touched." Brenda Winstone's shoes clinked on the stone walkway around the roof. The wooden door to the stairwell made a loud *CLANK* as she slammed it shut. *That's not good.* "I thought that the great Mina Wilde would forget all about the people whose lives she ruined."

"You ruined your own life when you decided to murder your husband and Ginny Button because they were having that affair."

"Harold's death wasn't my fault. None of it was! They made me do it with their torrid affair. Ginny was having the child that should have been mine. It was all going to work out perfectly. I was going to be the mother I'd always dreamed of being, but instead, I've been locked away with a bunch of terrifying psychopaths, and I haven't got to see a single child."

"Weren't you in..."

"...the Crixley Institution? Why yes. If you knew where I was, why didn't you send flowers?" Brenda's voice dripped with malice. "Since you remember me so fondly."

Of course. I vaguely recalled radio reports and headlines in the Argleton Gazette this week about a patient who escaped from Crixley. If I hadn't been so distracted, I might have thought to look up the name of that patient.

If the guys had told me about someone leaving threatening notes about the wedding, we might have been able to put two and two together.

Because of course, Brenda Winstone hadn't gone to prison. I knew that. I'd watched the papers about her case after we found her husband, the famous historian Harold Winstone, carved up and shoved in her hallway closet.

"You ruined my life, and you got to keep being free and living with those doting men of yours. That's not fair, and I believe the world should be fair. So I've come to make sure that you don't get your happily ever after." Brenda chuckled lightly. "I've been having so much fun since I escaped. I've been living in that bothy on Cynthia's land, and I stole some uniforms from her staff so I could come and go in the house as I please. I even walked right up to your men a couple of times, but of course they were too distracted to even recognise me. And Cynthia doesn't notice the help. Well, I helped myself. I intercepted that delivery and cut up your chair covers, but then I realized that you had Morrie's endless coffers and all these villagers giving you free things because they all worship the ground you walk on, so I knew I had to step up my plans. My roommate in Crixley showed me how to spoof phones, so after I heard Mabel shouting her mouth off at the pub about the chocolate delivery and the security having the day off, I lured Iwan to the loading bay, gave him a little tap on the head, and made sure that Heathcliff took the blame for his murder. I thought you'd call things off after I got rid of the only celebrant who'd agree to marry you, that you'd see how wrong it was that you got to have three husbands when some of us have none, but nothing stops Mina Wilde, does it? And then your men found my bothy, so I had to change my plans. I knew I couldn't get inside the wedding, so I knocked out one of the limo drivers this morning, borrowed her uniform, and showed up for her shift instead."

"You were the woman with the croaky voice?" It wasn't from the cigarettes. It was Brenda trying to disguise her voice.

"Yes. I was going to drive you somewhere peaceful after the ceremony and dispatch you. But when I saw you running away from the ceremony, I knew that finally, the good Lord was shining on me. This was my chance. So I drove you back to the village, which is practically empty as everyone is at Lachlan Hall. And I followed you. I thought you'd go back to Nevermore Bookshop, but you came up here, the same place where I got rid of that harlot who was trying to lead my Harold astray. That's a sign! If I get rid of you, I'll get Harold back, and everything will be fine again."

"Brenda, wait—"

I saw her shadow move and threw up my hands, but it was hard to block a blow coming for you when you can't see it.

Something slammed into the side of my face, sending my back against the roof. Oscar's harness ripped from my hand. Ancient tiles cracked beneath me. My arm scraped along the sharp edge of a slate roof tile, opening a cut that stung like hell. My head spun, and pain bloomed behind my eyes.

A dark shape loomed over me.

"Another thing I learned from my roommate at Crixley," Brenda said with a smirk. "How to throw a punch."

Oscar growled behind me. I struck out with a fist, but I was disoriented and blind AF. My punch only glanced off her arm.

Rough hands grabbed my shoulders and yanked me up,

spinning me around and slamming me against the stone parapet. Brenda leaned in close. "Say goodbye, Mina Wilde."

A scream tore from my throat as she shoved me over the wall.

CHAPTER 31
MINA

Time slowed down.

Air rushed around me. My legs wheeled and my arms clawed thin air, desperate to find something to cling to. As time slowed enough for me to contemplate the horrible death waiting for me in the church parking lot below, a hundred precious memories bloomed in my mind.

Heathcliff finding me hiding in a bathroom after some woman made comments about me looking too closely at the breakfast buffet. "Don't be driven low by petty people and their prejudice and hatred," he'd growled, clenching his hands into tight fists, so incensed on my behalf that I half-feared what he might do to them. "Don't take all that rage and turn it inward, until you hate yourself so much you become incapable of feeling anything else. You're no monster, Mina. This path is not for you. I'd leave you before I drag you down into the darkness with me."

Morrie lowering a blindfold over my eyes, telling me that I was the bravest person he'd ever met. "You fear the darkness. Not just the darkness that may eventually become your world, but also the darkness you see inside me. Inside Heathcliff and

Quoth, too. But you fear your own darkness most of all." He leaned forward, pressing his lips against my forehead. He lingered there, the heat of his lips searing through my doubts. "Maybe if you learn that the darkness is nothing to fear, then you'll be able to unleash all that Mina fury I know is hidden inside."

Stepping into Quoth's attic room and seeing a painting of myself on his easel. The woman in the image had my features, but she looked less like a hot mess in her flatmate's borrowed tartan trousers and more like the heroine from a gothic romance book, all sweeping hair and come-to-bed eyes. The soft colors around her face brought out her delicate features. On her shoulder sat a raven, its head turned toward her, utterly adoring. The first time I'd ever felt that I was someone who could be *adored.*

Heathcliff, Morrie, Quoth, I'm so sorry.

I wanted to be your wife.

I was afraid, but I'm not anymore.

I love you.

I braced myself for the splat, the pain, the end of it all. Instead, a whoosh of air surrounded me.

Something silken touched my skin, wrapping around me. And the whatever-it-was carried me up, up, up, my body reeling from the sudden change in acceleration and direction.

Have I already hit the ground? Have I died, and I'm being escorted to heaven by an angel? But that doesn't make sense, because I've already died once and it involved a bright light and the poet Dante...

"Mina, are you..." a voice choked out.

Not an angel.

Quoth.

He held me wrapped in one wing, the way he did during our dancing practice. His cheek pressed against mine. My feet hung free beneath us as he used his other wing to keep us midair

My heart was still hammering against my chest, but despite the cold air, a warmth spread through my body – a fire that belonged to Quoth.

I thought, in that moment, that the world had been made so we could find each other within it. How else could I explain his presence, his steadiness, his protection?

Quoth dipped his wing, and over the feathered tip, I could just make out the shape of the steeple against the bright sky. And the sound of Mrs. Winstone yelling, and some more quacking, and Oscar barking, and Heathcliff shouting. "I've got her. Get the coppers."

"So they can send her back to that place that let her run free?" Morrie shouted back. "I don't think so. I have plans for this woman and they involve splinters underneath her fingernails and—argh, don't attack me, you stupid bird! I'm not the villain in this story!"

"QUACK!"

Panic seized me. "Morrie? Heathcliff? Are they…"

"They're perfectly safe." Quoth pressed his cheek against mine. His tears ran over my skin. "Well, they have neutralized Brenda Winstone, but I think James Pond is trying to help. And as we learned today, no one is safe from a horny drake."

I heard a scuffle, Heathcliff yelling, and more quacking.

"Quoth?"

"Mina."

"I'm sorry—"

"You have nothing to be sorry for. We should have told you everything. But you're alive, and you will never be more precious to me than you are right now. Let's get you back on the ground."

I almost told him no, that I wanted to fly around a little

more, nestled in the safety of his wings and the warmth of his embrace. But he kissed the top of my head with such tenderness that tears spilt from my eyes, and set me down on the soft grass in the church graveyard.

As soon as he retracted his wings, my legs collapsed. He caught me in his arms. Quoth's tears mingled with mine. "Mina, I'm so so sorry. We should have told you about the notes sooner."

"Yes, you should have."

I could hear people shouting and car doors slamming as the churchyard filled with police and guests from our wedding, but I didn't care about any of that. My whole world had shrunk to this beautiful man holding me.

"It wasn't that we thought you couldn't handle it. It's the opposite – we knew you'd immediately leap into mystery-solving mode. You'd have thrown yourself into figuring out who left the notes, and we thought this time you deserved to have everything solved *for* you. We were trying to give a gift to the woman who has already given us everything."

He nuzzled against me, his hair falling over us in a curtain.

"If I'd been involved, we would have figured things out much earlier. I hope you've learned your lesson," I whispered into his shoulder. "But I'm sorry I ran away. I've been all twisted up inside about the book launch and feeling inadaquete. When I thought you didn't trust me to handle the fact that someone was after me, it felt the same as when Jen told me that my books weren't 'relatable.' I overreacted. And I felt awful standing there, knowing this person had killed before and that all our friends were in danger. I couldn't do it, but I ran instead of talking to you."

"I have to tell you about the book launch." Quoth smiled. "It's all back on."

My heart stuttered. "It's…what?"

"That's what I was doing yesterday. I called those people Marjorie recommended. They're blindness and disability influencers. They have huge social media accounts that advocate for disability representation, and they're both coming along to cover your book *and* bringing a bunch of their followers with them! I ordered some catering from a place Oliver recommended, and Morrie helped me bribe the printer to do a last-minute print run. Four boxes. I hope you don't mind, but they don't include any of your recent edits, but I think at this stage you were just shifting commas around as an excuse."

"Aw, Quoth, you...I can't believe..."

"That's the kind of thing a husband does for his wife." His words caught in his throat. "That is, if you still want to be my wife?"

"*Our* wife," Morrie corrected him. He and Heathcliff slammed into us, crushing me in a fierce embrace.

"Mina, I'm so sorry. This is my fault and mine alone," Heathcliff's voice choked. He pressed his cheek against mine, and it was wet with tears. "Please, don't leave me in the abyss without you. I'll spend the rest of my life making this up to you, if only you'll consider marrying us—"

Fresh tears flowed freely down my cheeks. "Of course I still want to marry you. But our whole wedding is ruined..."

"Not the *whole* wedding," Morrie said cheekily. "Just the parts the duck ate."

"I bet we can do something about—argh!" Heathcliff leapt away. "Keep that beast away from me!"

"QUACK?"

"That's James Pond!" I said. "I think he stowed away in the limo."

"QUACK QUACK."

James was waddling away from us. I broke free of my fiancés and followed him.

"Mina, I don't think you should wander around by yourself." Quoth jogged after me. "The ambulance is coming to check you out. You've got a nasty cut on your arm and—"

"QUACK."

I stalked James behind a row of overgrown gravestones. "He's got something in his mouth. I just need to—Quoth, help!"

"QUAAAACK!"

My birdie lunged forward just as James Pond rounded on me, trapping the bird beneath him. He pressed James' back lightly into the ground so he couldn't move, and pulled the object from his beak. "This is a piece of fabric from our waistcoats. So James was the one who ate the holes in them. And I bet you were the one who destroyed the wedding cake, too."

"Brenda didn't claim either of those things," I said, shuddering at the memory of meeting Brenda on the roof. "She said that she cut up the chair covers, spoofed Heathcliff's phone, and killed Iwan. And today, she was pretending to be the limo driver so she could drive me somewhere secret after the ceremony and...and..."

"That's not going to happen," Heathcliff said fiercely. "She's going back where she came from, with stronger locks this time."

"At least this explains why the cake was smeared all around Oliver's kitchen," Morrie said.

I pointed to James' impressive webbed feet. "He probably chased some poor girl duck inside. James, you horny bastard!"

Quoth's next words were cut off by the wail of sirens as an ambulance and more police tore into the parking lot. Quoth placed his arm around me and led me over to where the ambulance had parked. They pulled me up onto a stretcher and started to treat the cut on my arm, which had splashed blood all over the front of my dress, and check me over for other wounds.

"Step aside," said Maisie from the crowd of journalists who

were trying to get to us. "Mina's my friend, and she's not talking to anyone else. Mina, are you okay?"

"I'm fine," I told her. "Thanks to my guys. They saved me. But be careful if you go over near those graves, because there's a certain yellow duck who is horny AF and he wants you to know about it."

"James Pond?" Maisie dropped her reporter's recorder onto the grass and ran towards him. "I thought I'd lost you! I looked everywhere at Lachlan Hall. How did you get back to the village?"

"QUACK!"

"I can't believe you found him. I was so certain that I'd never see him again, and then he showed up at Lachlan Hall, but I lost him in the chaos and I thought he'd been trampled..." She hugged James to her chest.

"I think that James Pond has been trying to find a girl-friend," I said. "That's why he cut himself out of his cage, and he's been terrorizing the whole village and trying to ruin my wedding."

"Your wedding!" Maisie stood up abruptly. "Oh, Mina, I'm so so sorry. You're supposed to be getting married right now, and instead..."

"Oh, we're still getting married," a deep voice behind me said. Heathcliff.

"We can't get married now," I said. "Everything at Lachlan Hall is ruined. All of Quoth's decorations, the food..."

"Says who?" Heathcliff whispered back. "Do you still want to marry us?"

"Of course, but..."

"Then you get checked out by the paramedics, speak to Hayes, and let us take care of the rest." Heathcliff reluctantly unwrapped me from his arms and grabbed Morrie and Quoth.

"Come on, you two. Stop lounging around. We've got a wedding to save."

CHAPTER 32

MINA

Hayes had me change out of my ruined wedding dress so they could run forensics on it. Wilson brought me her gym clothes to change into, and once I was no longer bloody and had been checked over by the paramedics and pronounced fine, I sat on a bench in the graveyard and gave Hayes a rundown of everything that happened on the church roof.

Well, mostly everything. I left out the bit about flying with Quoth, and told Hayes that he'd helped me back down the stairs. If Hayes or anyone else had seen a long-haired guy with human-sized raven wings rescue me from midair, then they were keeping it to themselves.

We pieced the whole story together, how Brenda Winstone had seen my wedding announcement in the paper that she'd been allowed to read at the Crixley Institution, how she'd escaped and used her knowledge of Lachlan Hall from when she was friends with Cynthia to hide out on the estate and infiltrate the staff. How she'd tried to frame Heathcliff for Iwan's murder, but when that didn't work, she'd decided to kidnap me after the ceremony. How James Pond's activities had confused Heathcliff, Morrie, and Quoth into thinking all the incidents were related. How Morrie had checked out all the criminals I'd put behind bars but had forgotten about Brenda because she'd gone to Crixley instead of prison.

"I'm so sorry, Mina." Hayes put away his notepad. He sounded sad. "I failed in my job to protect you."

"It's really okay."

"It's not. I know that we haven't always agreed with the way you've inserted yourself into police business, but I want you to know that I admire the way you stick up for people and try to see every side of a story. You know, if you ever get tired of being a bookstore owner, you'd make a great private detective."

I beamed. "Thanks. That means a lot."

"Don't tell DS Wilson I said that."

"I heard my name." Wilson approached us. "Are you finished with Mina now?"

Hayes patted my knee. "I think that I've got everything I need. You're a free woman now, unlike Brenda Winstone, who won't have such lax security around her again. When we took her away, she was yelling about she pushed you off the roof and a giant bird man saved you. She's even more disturbed than we thought."

"Thank you, Inspector." I stood up, clutching Oscar's harness. My weary bones were ready to return home to Nevermore and have a long shower.

"Not so fast, Wilde," Wilson hissed.

"But Inspector Hayes said he was finished with me—"

"He may be, but I've been sent with rather specific instructions to get you to the Rose & Wimple for your wedding."

Perplexed, I allowed Wilson to slip her arm through mine. I noticed that we took the backstreets, walking briskly past Maisie's house and around the corner to arrive at the pub via the back entrance near the old stables, instead of the much quicker route across the village green.

Wilson bustled me upstairs to where Jo and Bree were practically bouncing off the walls of a small hallway, still wearing their bridesmaid's dresses, which miraculously seemed to have survived the carnage, although I couldn't see them well enough to judge.

"We're here to get you dressed," Bree announced proudly.

"But I don't understand. My wedding dress was ruined—"

"Come on." Jo grabbed my hand and yanked me inside. "You're not going to *believe* this."

They herded me into the tiny hotel room. All the lights were on, and a couple of extra lamps had been brought in to help me see. I could make out the shape of a dressmakers' form in the middle of the room, and someone was hunched over it. A familiar voice grumbled about poor materials and tight deadlines.

A voice I never thought I'd hear again.

Marcus Ribald.

The infamous New York designer who'd fired me from my internship after my friend Ashley told him about my retinitis pigmentosa diagnosis.

What is he doing here?

"Mina?" Jo squeezed my arm. "Are you okay? You've gone all pale."

"Mina, there you are!" The figure barrelled toward me, and Marcus leaned in to plant a customary air kiss on each cheek. I was too stunned to move. "The bride herself arrives, and just in time, for I am putting the finishing touches on your dress."

"My...dress?"

He took my hand and guided me towards the dressmakers' form. "Mina, I know you're a little surprised to see me. The truth is, I'm a little surprised to be here myself."

"But...but...but...*how?*"

"I was on the way to Crookshollow for a meeting about an upcoming fashion exhibition when my car was nudged off the road and my driver directed to walk back to civilization. Your fiancé slid into the driver's seat, introduced himself as James Moriarty, and explained that we were taking a detour so I could help you with your wedding dress."

"He...what?" I couldn't comprehend this.

Did Marcus Ribald just save my wedding dress?

Did Hayes *lie* to me about taking it for evidence collection?

"Morrie and I have become fast friends in that short but terrifying drive." Marcus' voice trembled a little. *Ah yes, being Morrie's 'friend' can be a dangerous business.* "He's made me see that I was wrong to let you go from the internship. You had so much talent, but I've seen this business chew up hundreds of talented people and spit them out again, and none of them had your disability to contend with. I didn't think that you would be able to handle the workload."

"I would have liked the chance to sink or swim on my own merits," I said. Jo squeezed my hand.

"I should have given you that chance. I am truly sorry."

This was *surreal.* All the nights I'd spent crying over what this man did, how he'd chosen me from hundreds of applicants because of my talent and then dismissed me without a thought once he found out that I was *less than.* And now he was *here*, and I had dreamed of all the things I wanted to say to him.

But I didn't. I didn't want to yell at him or make him pay any more than Morrie had already done. I felt...calm.

You're the one who lost out, Marcus. Not me.

Marcus squeezed my upper arm. "If you decide to continue in fashion, I'd love to have you back."

I beamed. "Thanks, but I'm actually pretty happy with how everything turned out."

"Oh, that's good," he sounded relieved. "Morrie will be *so* pleased to hear that. Now, shall I take your hand and show you your dress?"

I nodded. Marcus placed his hand over mine and ran my fingers over the garment.

"This particular challenge tested all of my skills. The hem was ruined, there was an enormous hole singed through every layer of the skirt, and there were a few unsightly duck-related stains, so I've done a quick dye job, raised the hemline, and given the corset a bit of heavy metal bling, and I think with the red Docs your friends insist that you want to wear—" I couldn't tell if his tone is admiring or derisive "—I think this will work. That police officer even rescued your veil from the churchyard, so I've dyed that to match. I know if anyone can pull off a black wedding dress, it's Mina Wilde."

"Damn right," Bree said. "Mina, you were *born* to wear this dress."

I ran my hands over the skirt, admiring the way Marcus had transformed the ragged destruction of the fire into a feature of the dress. The skirt now hung in different length panels, the ends rough and frayed and completely punk rock. He'd added spikes and studs to the corset and made matching wrist cuffs.

This dress was something that Amy Lee or Simone Simons would wear in a music video.

This was why Marcus Ribald was a fashion *genius*.

A lump formed in my throat.

"I love it."

"As well you should." Marcus leaned in and kissed both my cheeks. "Now put it on and get out there before your fiancé comes back and makes good on one of his creative threats."

Grinning, I kissed Marcus back. He slunk out of the room, closing the door behind him. I practically danced out of my clothes, and Jo and Bree laced me back into my corset. I couldn't stop touching all the spikes and studs, and the cool ragged hem. This dress was so much more *me* than the poofy white princess one I had before.

"I can't wait for you to see what else the guys have done," Bree said as she laced up my scuffed old red Docs. "I don't know how they pulled this off in a couple of hours."

"I do." Jo's voice choked up. "There's nothing those men won't do for you, Mina."

They finished lacing me up, then Jo went to work on my makeup, wiping off the glam look that Cynthia's artist had given me that morning and replacing it with heavy eyeliner, deep red lips, and sparkles from my own stash. Bree pulled my hair back and affixed my black veil with a comb that Marcus had done up with more spikes and studs.

"You're all ready to go," Jo stood back. "Now we just have to wait for—"

A knock pounded at the door.

"There she is. Smiles on, ladies!"

"Mina, there you are!" Mum burst into the room. "We have to get your downstairs—Oh, no, what happened to your beautiful dress?"

"Hey, Mum." I did a twirl. "Don't you love it?"

"I suppose it will have to do." She leaned in and kissed my cheek. "You look like you're going to marry a vampire, but you also look *beautiful*."

"Thanks, Mum." A rush of love for her coursed through my body. Mum drove me crazy, but she also raised me all by herself, and even when she didn't understand me, she always supported me and made sure I was surrounded by love. "Will you walk me down the aisle? I know I said before that I wanted to walk by myself, but I changed my mind. I don't even know if there *is* an aisle, but..."

"I'd be honored, darling." Mum's voice cracked. "And of

course there's an aisle. Your boys have outdone themselves. We have to go! Everyone has gathered!"

"Wait, my bridesmaids!"

"We're ready." Jo gave her lips a final swipe with my lipstick and smoothed down the front of her dress (which upon closer inspection I realized had also got the Marcus Ribald treatment – it was now artfully slashed and studded). Bree stuffed a package of tissues into her bra and waved goodbye to the ghost of an old publican who was apparently in the corner of the room, and we lined up and snapped a quick selfie.

Mum slid her arm in mine and practically dragged me and Oscar down the narrow steps and around the side of the pub. Dusk was starting to fall, the lack of light making my vision worse than usual. Luckily, my dress no longer dragged on the ground for me to trip over. As we neared the village green, I heard the distinct sounds of people shuffling around and a cello quartet warming up their instruments.

Maisie ran over, and Mum told her that we were in position. A moment later, the music changed to my entrance song. I gripped Mum's arm as we wandered a little around the corner and Jo and Bree prepared to start their slow walk across...

I blinked as the village green came into my view. "Oh, wow, it's *beautiful*."

Jo's arm went around my neck, and she pulled me close. "You're a lucky woman, Mina Wilde. If I was into dick, I'd be insanely jealous."

The entire green was lit up with strings of fairy lights. Every shop window, every park bench, street lamp, and every outdoor table at the Rose & Wimple had been outlined with twinkling lights. In the center, an archway made of bright-coloured Chinese lanterns stole the show. Everywhere I looked, my eyes delighted in the colors and sparkles. It was like a secret, magical world that only I appreciated.

Jo and Bree set off on their cue, their dresses sweeping through the grass, making the crowd ooh with appreciation for Marcus' handiwork.

"How did they…"

"Heathcliff went around to every person in the village and demanded they hand over their fairy lights. Remember that fairy light store in Grimdale that went out of business last year and had that half-off sale that caused the dual carriageway to be blocked for six hours? Well, because of that, everyone had dozens of strings gathering dust in their cupboards, and no one says no to Heathcliff when he looks at you like *that*. So lights were brought and Quoth took the lanterns left over from the Chinese Lantern festival and arranged everything."

Oh, Quoth.

Of course he did this. It had all been done with an artist's eye. As I clutched my mum's arm, my eyes roamed over every building around the square, their edges, doors, windows and posts all marked out with rows of twinkling lights. For tonight, I could see the village again, only now it was more magical than ever.

"Are you ready?" Mum squeezed my hand, her voice husky with emotion.

"Mum, are you crying?"

"I just want you to know that I'm so proud of you." Her words stuck in her throat as she struggled to hold herself together. "Not just because you're getting married, but because of everything that you've achieved. When you came back from New York with your diagnosis, I didn't know what to do. I was so afraid for you. But I should have known that you'd land on your feet. You're always so creative and resourceful."

I beamed as my own throat choked up. "I wonder where I get that from?"

"Well, your father was a poet—"

"No, Mum, I got it from you, the creative, ambitious, infuriating woman who raised me." I wrapped my arms around her. "There's something I want you to know, too. I'm proud to be your daughter."

"Oh, Mina."

The music swelled again, signaling my cue. With Mum clutching one arm and Oscar tugging gently on his harness in the other, I took my first step down the aisle.

CHAPTER 33
MINA

I expected time to freeze, for my mind to race with a million questions about whether I'd made the right decision, whether I was too young, whether we should have waited to have our perfect wedding at Lachlan Hall.

But this *was* the perfect wedding, because my three men made it for me, and everyone I loved was here.

Because it was *impossible*, and yet, here we were...

Because ever since I'd walked back through the door of Nevermore Bookshop, my life had been touched by magic, and why should my wedding day be any different?

My feet moved of their own accord, practically sprinting down the aisle. I didn't care about the *snap snap snap* of the photographer, or what people were saying about my dress. I just wanted to get to them. I wanted to be in their arms.

I wanted to be their *wife*.

As I moved towards the arch, the three blurry figures standing beneath the lights resolved into three familiar, impossible men.

Heathcliff, Morrie, and Quoth all waiting for me.

Morrie stepped up and took my hand, untangling me from

Oscar's lead. He leaned in and whispered something to my mother's ear that had her chuckling.

"You take good care of her, James," my mother scolded. "You may be a scallywag, but if you hurt her, I'll monogram my initials on your bollocks."

"As terrifying as the prospect is, I don't think you'll need to make good on your threats," Morrie said. "Mina is more precious to me than an entire criminal empire. Hey, gorgeous, you made it."

"*We* made it." My chest fluttered. Morrie pulled me in close, his lean body warm against mine as he laid a soft, tender kiss on the top of my head. I closed my eyes and steadied my pulse against his.

After everything we've been through, including a murderer trying to keep us apart, we made it.

Morrie's long fingers closed around mine. "I see you have a new dress."

"Mmmm." I leaned against his shoulder as he led me and Oscar up the two short steps of the platform usually used for giving out the prizes at the village fete. "Thanks to you and your newly forged friendship with my old boss."

"Hey, he may be a slimy weasel who wouldn't know a good thing if it smacked him around the head with a wet fish, but the man has *style*." Morrie ran his fingers along the studs on the corset. "I wonder if he'd make me a new suit for the honeymoon. Perhaps one impervious to dinosaur teeth…"

"He'd probably do anything you ask, since he's *terrified* of you."

"Of me?" Morrie said innocently. "But I'm a harmless little kitten. Here's Heathcliff."

Morrie placed my hand into Heathcliff's large, rough palm. His fingers closed around mine, and a lump rose in my throat.

"I can't believe you did all this for me," I breathed, my fingers squeezing his. His hand in mine felt like home.

He brushed his lips over my forehead, cupping my face in his hands and resting against me. His stubble grazed my skin. "I would do this a hundred times over," he whispered against me. "I would dress up in silly outfits and learn to dance and have arguments with Oliver over cake decorations for the rest of my days if it made you smile."

"Luckily for the world, I'm pretty easy to please. *You* make me smile, just by being you."

He smiled then, his lips moving over my skin so I could feel it. A rare, wondrous Heathcliff smile. A smile that felt like sunshine where it touched me.

Heathcliff stepped back, and there was my Quoth, his black hair brushed to a high sheen, swept back at the sides and tied with a ribbon that sparkled with the iridescent colors of his feathers.

"You are beautiful," he whispered as he took my hand and spun me beneath his arm. "I can't believe you're mine. I'm dreaming a dream that no mortal has ever dreamed before. How did I get to be so lucky to love and be loved by you?"

"You were my ebony bird beguiling my sad fancy into smiling," I said to him as he caught me against his chest. "Since we're quoting from your creator. You've always been beside me, always understood me, even when I didn't understand myself. You promised to watch over me, and you've always kept your promise, even when it tore you apart." I kissed the tip of his nose. "I'm so excited to be your wife."

"Alright now," Pax, Bree's boyfriend and our new celebrant, shoved us apart. "Let's get this wedding underway, before the gods curse us with another evil duck."

I thought that I'd be so overcome by it all that I wouldn't stop crying. I usually cried during emotional moments. But not today, not when I was marrying my three best friends. I beamed all the way through Bree's boyfriend Edward's terrible poem about love. I laughed as Heathcliff vowed to finally tell me where he kept his secret chocolate stash and Morrie vowed to occasionally let me win at chess. My face hurt from smiling as the three of them slid their ring on my finger.

My whole body glowed with warmth as each one of them took me in their arms and kissed me until I was drunk with happiness.

Reader, I married them.

CHAPTER 34
QUOTH

Once the ceremony was done, everyone in the village crowded around to hug us. By the time Mrs. Ellis and her friends were done with us, we smelled of lamb's wool and hyacinths and our organs were all smushed out of place.

While Lydia Bennet barked orders at the team transforming the green for the reception, the four of us snuck off to Nevermore Bookshop, where Hayes had set up a photoshoot. Our official photographer had bailed after James Pond cracked her lens with his beak, but it turned out that when Hayes wasn't solving crimes and arresting Mina or Heathcliff for stuff they didn't do, he was an amateur photographer. He mostly shot nature photography but he thought he could do some decent wedding portraits. We posed against the bookshelves and took shots of Mina reading in the old leather chair with the three of us looming behind her like the villains we are. Then we took a bunch of silly group shots with Bree and Jo and Mina's mother and Mrs. Ellis over in the graveyard, because of course we did.

After the photography was done, we returned to the green just as Lydia finished arranging tables in regimental rows and

Richard was bringing out platters of sausage rolls, fish and chips, mini hot dogs, and pork belly sliders. Someone had even thoughtfully provided a Quoth-platter of all my favourites – nuts, grain mixes, dried berries, and little chunks of meat. Cynthia brought over a few trays of fancy hors d' oeuvres she managed to rescue from James Pond, and a table in the corner groaned under the weight of several cheesecakes.

"That's a lot of cheesecakes," Mina said as Morrie read out the selection. "One might guess it was a lifetime supply."

"It turns out, no one won that radio competition, so Smooth Loamshire decided to donate the lifetime supply of cheesecakes to a worthy cause," Morrie grinned as he filled up a plate of food for Mina.

"Oh, they did, did they? Out of the kindness of their hearts?" I raised an eyebrow at him. "They weren't prompted by a certain Napoleon of Crime with a sweet tooth?"

"Don't worry, birdie, I did everything *non-violently*." Morrie licked cheesecake off his fingers. "Mmmm, these are delicious."

Morrie filled up a plate of food for Mina while she dragged me over to where the pub band were setting up.

"Got any requests for your first dance?" Oliver asked. He was the drummer.

"Oh, hell yes." Mina grabbed me around the waist as she whispered a song into his ear.

When the band struck up the first bars of The Doors 'People are Strange,' everyone in the crowd went wild. Mina wrapped her arms around me, and her green eyes reflected the shimmering fairy lights as I spun her around the makeshift dance floor. The magical waters of Meles sparkled behind her eyes.

All around me, our friends clapped and cheered. I dipped Mina low, laughing as she tripped over my feet on the way back up. My wings itched against my skin, but I didn't unfurl them.

For the first time, I didn't want to hide away.

Why would I?

Mina Wilde was my *wife*.

There was nothing more strange or wonderful than that.

I wanted to paint it on my skin, sing it into a microphone, shout it from the tallest rooftop (well, considering the tallest rooftop in the village was the bell tower where I rescued Mina just in time, maybe not that).

I couldn't believe how lucky I was.

"Quoth," Mina clung to me as the band changed to a Jethro Tull cover. "I love dancing with you, but if I'm going to embarrass myself all night, I need a drink and some more cheesecake."

"One thing this wedding isn't short of is cheesecake." I looped her arm in mine. We wove through the crowd on our way to the dessert table. Every few steps, we were stopped by someone wishing us well, or Mina wanted to check out the platters of mini beef and Guinness pies and haddock and chips, and the stalls people in the village had set up. There was Mrs. Ellis' knitting club taking bets on a 'knit-off' between two octogenarians that looked like it was about to turn violent. A long line of people clamored for Sylvia Blume to read their fortunes. In the corner, Mina's mother had set up her monogram machines in a stall and was helping a bunch of kids make their own avant-garde handkerchiefs. She'd even managed to program her machine to embroider the quick sketch of a raven I'd given her.

We found Heathcliff and Morrie over at the dessert table, chatting with Sherlock and David Winter, whose entwined hands suggested the Great Toothbrush Battle had been well and truly settled.

"Now this is my kind of wedding feast." Juice dribbled down Heathcliff's chin as he bit into a slider. Morrie reached across him and wiped it away. Heathcliff glared at him, but he didn't break Morrie's fingers.

"I have to admit, you did an amazing job, Lord Grumble-bum," Morrie said. "You missed your calling as an event planner. The next time the League of Literary Villains hosts our annual awards dinner, you should run it."

"The League of Wassit?" Mina asked.

"Shhh." Morrie held his finger to her lips. "Forget I said anything, gorgeous."

"This wasn't exactly the wedding I planned," Heathcliff said. "But I think it's turned out even better."

"I couldn't agree more." Mina snuggled into my armpit as we watched Inspector Hayes and Victor Frankenstein set up a bunch of fireworks on the village green. "I feel so loved and held by everybody tonight. I can't believe you managed to get the whole village to pull this off so quickly."

"You *are* rather beloved around here, gorgeous," Morrie said. "And not just by us. You touch people. You make them feel like they are special and interesting and worthy of love and respect. I know it's wretchedly sentimental of me to say, but you inspire people to do better and be better. The way you rose from ruination to make this beautiful life, I think even a phoenix would be jealous."

I couldn't have said it better myself.

Mina fell silent. I thought she was just soaking it all in, but then she said, "I don't think this is all for me."

Morrie touched her shoulder. "Come now, you're the wife of James Moriarty, I won't hear of any false modesty."

She squeezed me tight. "I mean, our friends didn't do this just for me. The three of you need to face facts – you're just as beloved as I am around here."

"You take that back," Heathcliff growled, but his dark eyes had a sparkle to them. Even grumpy, lonesome Heathcliff had found his place in the world, and all because of the remarkable woman sitting on my knee, stuffing her sixth pork belly slider of the evening betwixt her glorious lips.

When Mina returned to Argleton a year ago, her spirit was bruised, and she was looking for where she belonged. We all were.

She split us all open, showed us we were worth all the work of piecing our broken hearts together again, that in this crazy, wild world, there was someone that fit so perfectly into us that all the words from all the greatest writers that have ever lived wouldn't be able to capture the *rightness* of being with her.

Because of her, I found my place in the world.

This raven has found *home*.

CHAPTER 35

MINA

"Isn't our wife beautiful?" Quoth said, sliding his hands up my thighs, pushing the fabric of my black dress to the side.

Our wife.

I would never get tired of those words falling from his lips.

I didn't know how late it was. We danced and ate and drank and laughed and sang along with every terrible rock cover the band threw at us until the mayor came along and said that we had to shut everything down or he'd be forced to issue us with a police warning, and Hayes didn't look in any state to do it. I'd started to help Mum tear down the decorations, but Heathcliff hoisted me into his arms and marched me back to Nevermore Bookshop, the other two jogging after him.

Quoth had unlocked the door and Morrie moved ahead of us, turning on lights and lamps so Heathcliff wouldn't trip, narrating in his rich, fictive voice all the things he wanted to do to me, now that I was his wife. Quoth followed behind, leading Oscar and putting him to bed with some kibble.

Heathcliff carried me up both flights of stairs like I was a feather, and laid me upon our bed. I don't remember the moment we went from not touching to touching. All I knew was that magic hung thick in the air as the three of them converged on me, the star in the center of their universe, their scents mingling together, their touch fire and water and life and death.

It was everything and it was nothing, leaving behind my old self, shedding the skin of a Mina who didn't fit anymore, and becoming anew in their arms. It was stepping through the doorway of home and finding myself beside a warm fire. *Their fire.*

Morrie laid kisses on my lips like prayers, soft and reverent. Heathcliff unlaced my corset with an urgency that trembled in the air. When my breasts were free, he palmed them, his rough fingers stroking the nipples until I cried out.

Quoth undid the fastenings on my skirt and tugged it and my knickers over my thighs. Before I had a chance to breathe, he dived between my legs, his tongue finding the exact spot that drove me wild.

My three husbands held me, kissed me, worshiped me, their tongues and hands finding new ways to write their love for me.

My legs were already shaking under Quoth's expert tongue, my orgasm building as I pushed up my hips to meet his awaiting mouth.

My first orgasm came hard and fast, a release of pressure after a night of grinding against them on the dance floor, of stolen touches and increasingly intense kisses for our friends' cameras.

Morrie caught my strangled moans as Quoth dipped his tongue between my thighs, lapping up every part of my orgasm until I collapsed against them.

I reached out to Heathcliff, who stroked my nipples with his tongue. My fingers brushed the collar of his shirt, and the seam where Quoth had glued on his faux waistcoat after James Pond ate his way through the silk.

"Get these ridiculous shirts off, all of you," I whispered. "If I'm to be naked, it's only fair that my husbands should be, too."

My husbands.

I'll never get sick of saying that.

And I would never get sick of nights like this, the four of us together, conjuring magic and chasing away our demons.

Never have three men got undressed so fast. Morrie didn't even pause to fold his clothes. His belt buckle made a distinctive CLANG as it hit the wall, followed shortly after by his trousers and socks. The bed groaned as the three of them climbed on, crawling to me like men embarking upon *katabasis*.

Wrapping one arm around Morrie's neck and the other around Heathcliff, I leaned back into the headboard, my shoulders relaxing as I took in all of the pleasure and love surrounding me.

"We did it," Morrie said, his voice filled with wonder. "It took a long time, an eternity, but we made you ours."

"I think that I was always yours," I said. "I think that my whole life, I've been waiting for this moment."

"Then we'd better make it worth the wait," Heathcliff growled. His body vibrated with a restless energy, fighting the battle between his need to control and that feral, dangerous side of him, the side that wasn't all that dissimilar to a certain wild antihero born of the moors.

I was nearly torn apart by the need to know which one of him was mine tonight. I parted my legs, and his hand snaked between them, playing with me, teasing me, making me moan against Quoth's lips.

Morrie's long fingers sank into my hips as he lifted me and plopped me down on his shaft, cowgirl-style. I was so ready for him that he slid right in, filling me completely.

"Ride me, wife," Morrie commanded, his fingers digging in.

I obeyed, because no one can refuse James Moriarty when

he speaks with the tongue of a devil. I tossed my hair back and rode him, grinding my hips against his, forcing all kinds of animalistic sounds from his throat.

Hands explored my body as I drove down on Morrie, rolling my nipples, drawing circles on my back, kneading my arse. And then, a heavy, muscled chest pressed against my back just as a soft, warm head of a cock rubbed against my lips.

"Wife," Quoth whispered, his whole body shuddering as I opened my lips to take him in.

He tasted so sweet, my bird, my husband, sweet as a lifetime supply of cheesecake. I moaned as I took him deep, circling my tongue against his head before curling my lips around the length of his shaft.

Quoth's fingers tangled in my hair, and the sounds falling from his lips were anything *but* sweet and innocent.

Behind me, Heathcliff growled against my skin, his teeth scraping across my shoulder as he rubbed lube onto his fingers. Beneath me, Morrie squirmed with delight.

"I can't wait to feel you come when all three of us are inside you, wife," he said, leaning back on the pillows and putting his hands behind his head, as if he was just enjoying the show.

I panted, unsure how to answer. Could I take more than this?

"If I die of pleasure on my wedding night, you and Heathcliff and Quoth are going to be on the hook for my murder."

Morrie chucked. "I say it was worth it."

I tried to focus on drawing Quoth's length inside my mouth as Heathcliff slid his finger inside me, working slowly, relaxing me, preparing me. Morrie slowed his thrusts. He loved this part.

"Are you ready for me?" Heathcliff asked, his breath kissing my neck.

"I'm ready, husband."

"When you say that word, I just about come apart," he grunted as he thrust forward.

Even though we'd done this several times now, I was never fully prepared for the sensation of all three of them inside me, how spread and warm and held and amazing I felt. Heathcliff's length seated itself inside me, pressing against Morrie through the thin layer that separated them. My lips wrapped around Quoth, dragging him deeper, so deep that I gagged, wanting as much of him as I had of the others. I was greedy for all three of them.

Heathcliff and Morrie started to move. They'd developed a rhythm between them that was as much about them fucking each other as it was about me, a way for the two of them to connect through me. My nails dug into Morrie's shoulders. I couldn't move, couldn't think, all I could do was hold on while they drove into me.

My whole body lit up like a sparkler. That was the only way to describe the way the pleasure fizzled inside me and burst out through my skin.

I didn't know where my body ended and theirs began anymore; we were all connected, all one.

The first orgasm came more slowly this time. It danced green and orange lights in front of my eyes. But once I was there, the three of them held me in that liminal place, caring for me, whispering my name, worshiping me.

I lost track of the number of times I came. It felt more like one long, slow, continuous orgasm, a pleasure that crested like waves against a shore, relentless and rhythmic and eternal. It was only when Heathcliff let out a final thrust, his guttural moan shaking the bed, that I realized it was over, that Morrie had gone soft inside me, that I could taste Quoth's pleasure on my tongue.

The men moved around me, each one placing light kisses on

my forehead. Heathcliff wrapped his strong arms around me and pulled me down onto the bed, tucking me against his chest. Quoth brought a warm washcloth, and softly, lovingly cleaned between my legs and along my thighs. Morrie dug his long fingers into the soles of my feet, making short work of the pain of dancing all night.

"I don't know what souls are made of," Heathcliff murmured. "But yours and ours are the same."

"Aw, now that's not fair." I snuggled down into his embrace. "You read that in a book."

CHAPTER 36
MINA

"I don't know what you were worried about, dear." Mum handed me a glass of bubbles. "This book launch is a complete success. You couldn't fit any more people in the shop if you tried."

She wasn't wrong. The Events room was so packed that I was half afraid the fire department would shut us down, if they weren't all crowded around the makeshift bar Edward had set up on Heathcliff's desk, downing themed cocktails called 'The Raven' and 'Heathcliff's Revenge,' and 'The Reichenbach Tall.'

Everywhere, phones flashed as Majorie's disability influencer friends snapped their pics. Every few seconds I was pulled into another photo. And all around me, people had my book tucked under their arms or holding them out for me to sign.

My face hurt from smiling, but I didn't think I could stop if I tried.

This was an even better turnout than Danny Sledge's ill-fated book launch, and the best thing was, no one had been murdered.

Or maybe the best thing was that my book was out in the

world. I'd come this far. Whatever happened now was up to fate and magic, and I had a lot of that on my side.

"Thanks, Mum." I hugged her. "I can't believe how many people came on such short notice."

"This is amazing! You're going to be a star! You're going to sell more than that Ellie James Child person—"

EL James? Lee Child?

Sometimes it was better not to ask.

"—and I can finally move out of our flat and into the manor home with the kidney-shaped pool that I've always dreamed of."

"I don't know about that," I beamed. "But it *is* pretty wonderful to know that readers want books with characters like me."

"Maybe for your next book, you could add more about the Mum character," Mum said. "Maybe she could secretly inherit a fortune! I have so many ideas—"

"Mina, there you are!"

I turned towards Maisie's voice, grateful for the distraction from Mum's brilliant plot ideas. "Thank you so much for coming! How's James Pond doing?"

"A lot better now that I've got him a couple of female friends to keep him company." Maisie toasted my glass with hers. "Two lovely ladies I've named Hot Wings and Lady Featherston. Stanley helped me modify James' pen to suit them all. He's actually really lovely. Did you know he transformed his entire living room into an aviary for nursing injured birds back to health?"

I grinned. "Why no, I had no idea."

"It's true. I feel bad about accusing him of duck-napping James. And I feel awful that James Pond ruined your wedding. I can't believe that one horny duck could do so much damage."

"Me neither. But don't worry about it. James didn't ruin

anything. With the exception of poor Iwan's death, I truly believe that everything worked out exactly as it should have in the end."

I smiled as I listened to Heathcliff trying to get Edward to make him a triple-strength cocktail, and Morrie dragging Quoth around the room, telling everyone who'd listen that he drew the cover art.

"I'm relieved to hear it," Maisie said. "Listen, I have a favor to ask. I promise that it's not another case for you to solve."

"Good, because I think after James Pond, I'm ready to hang up my hat for good." I patted the stack of books beside me. "I want to write about murders, not experience them. What's the favor?"

"I brought along a couple of my friends tonight, and they all got copies of your book. We've been talking about how we don't have the time or motivation to read anymore, but having a book that we can read together has made us excited about reading again. We're thinking of starting a monthly book club where we get together and talk about our favorite smutty books and murder mysteries. Would you be willing to be a guest speaker next month? And maybe also let us host the club in Nevermore Bookshop?"

Her words came out in a nervous rush.

"I'd love that, but on one condition. That you let me be a member. I want to read smutty books and murder mysteries with you every month." I grinned. "And I already have some suggestions for titles."

"Yes, please. We'd love to have you! I can't wait for you to meet my friends. Although I must warn you, they're a little... odd."

I nodded in the vague direction of where I could hear Morrie. "You've seen who I'm married to. Odd will fit right in around here."

"Yes, that's good. They're a little obsessed with the supernatural. And true crime podcasts. One of them is convinced that Argleton is home to more than a couple of vampires."

"The only vampires around here are between the covers of books." *Since I got rid of Dracula, and we repaired the leaky pipes at Nevermore. And the time-travelling room isn't available for the public.*

I hope.

"Our working title is the 'The Nevermore Murder Club, Magic Circle, and Smutty Book Society.' We couldn't agree on smutty books or true crime, you see, so we decided to name it after both."

"I think that we're going to have a lot of fun."

"Are we now, gorgeous?" An arm flung over my shoulder, and Morrie's deep voice whispered against my ear. "What are we doing that's fun? Something devious, I hope. And can your friend join us?"

EPILOGUE

MINA

"Where is everyone?" I yelled, my fingers trembling as I gripped the door handle. "You have two minutes!"

"Arf!" Oscar added. He was sitting patiently beside me, squashed between my two large suitcases. It was difficult to pack for a surprise honeymoon when it could be anywhere the shop had existed throughout time. But at least I was packed, unlike Morrie, who was still tossing clothes out the door of our bedroom, or Heathcliff, who—

"I'm here. I've got everything I need." Heathcliff sauntered into the hall. He held up his flask before sliding it into the pocket of his woolen coat beside a battered paperback book.

"That's all your packing?"

"I've got this as well." Heathcliff opened the other flap of his coat, showing me the large sword strapped to his belt. "And I've got you, my wife. That's all I need."

"Mina, you have your toothbrush?" Quoth bustled in, dropping a backpack in front of the door. He consulted the list he'd made.

"I do, thanks, Mum."

"What about your bathing suit? Just in case Morrie's right and we somehow end up on a deserted island?"

"The bathing suit is packed."

"And what about that new toy I gave you as a wedding present?" Morrie asked as he came up behind me and slid his arms around my waist, his breath tickling my ear.

"Yes, 'Big Red' is safe in here." I patted my suitcase.

"I wish your father had given us more instructions," Morrie complained as he kicked his own enormous suitcase. "It's rather difficult to decide which suit will match the decor when one doesn't know where one is going. Did he say anything about what we'd encounter on the other side?"

"All he said was that if we stepped through the door at exactly 10:17AM, we'd have an experience we'd never forget."

"If I get eaten by a velociraptor, I won't forget," Heathcliff muttered.

"Arf," Oscar agreed.

"I'm sure that Homer wouldn't send us to our doom," Quoth said, not sounding sure at all.

"Is that the same Homer who wrote the *Iliad*, which rightfully should be retitled 'Achilles Fucks Shit Up'?" Morrie asked sweetly.

"Or perhaps, 'Hello, You Naughty Trojans, It's Murder Time,'" Heathcliff added.

"Or 'There is No Heterosexual Explanation for What Happens Next.'"

"On second thought, I think I'll just stay behind. I forgot that I left my birdcage open." Quoth sounded terrified.

I burst out laughing. This whole situation was ridiculous, and my three husbands were the most *ridiculous*. I wouldn't change a thing. This was what being married to three fictional villains meant – endless bickering, crazy adventures, and literary references that made your head spin.

My life would never be boring with them.

Heathcliff placed his hand over mine on the handle. He turned our hands together and leaned against the door, pushing it inwards a crack. "Are we ready for this? We don't know what we're walking into."

"I know," I grinned as all five of us stepped inside. "That's what makes it fun."

THE END

Return to Nevermore Bookshop for a brand new series. Devour book 1 of the The Nevermore Murder Club, Magic Circle, and Smutty Book Society soon.

What do you do when 3 hot, possessive ghosts want to jump your bones? Find out in Bree's series, the Grimdale Graveyard Mysteries, and enjoy cameos from your favourite characters from Nevermore Bookshop.

START NOW:
http://books2read.com/grimdale1

(Turn the page for a sizzling excerpt)

Can't get enough of Mina and her boys? Read a free alternative scene from Quoth's point-of-view along with other bonus scenes and extra stories when you sign up for the Steffanie Holmes newsletter.

EPILOGUE

http://www.steffanieholmes.com/newsletter

FROM THE AUTHOR

It's bittersweet to write the final words in Mina's story. On the one hand, I'm so filled with joy to give Mina and her fictional men their happily-ever-after. On the other, I'm not yet ready to leave behind a cute magical bookshop that filled my heart for so many years.

So, I'm not. You'll be getting a brand new series featuring all new characters and their magical book club and supernatural murder mystery society that operates out of Nevermore. You'll see lots of your favourite characters and meet some new book boyfriends. I can't wait!

And if you need something to help you deal with your Nevermore book hangover while you wait, I've got you covered. Check out the Grimdale Graveyard Mysteries series, where our heroine Bree is up to her ears in ghostly shenanigans with her harem of three possessive spirits. Book 1 is *You're So Dead to Me* and it's set in the same world as Nevermore, so you'll meet a few of your favourite characters: http://books2read.com/grim dale1

If you want to hang out and talk about all things Nevermore, get updates and a free book of cut scenes and bonus stories, you can join my newsletter – http://steffanieholmes.com/newsletter.

A portion of the proceeds from every Nevermore book sold go toward supporting Blind Low Vision NZ Guide Dogs, and I'm always sharing cute guide dog pictures and vids in my Facebook group.

I'm so happy you enjoyed this story! I'd love it if you wanted to leave a review on Amazon or Goodreads. It will help other readers to find their next read.

Thank you, thank you! I love you heaps! Until next time.

Steffanie

EXCERPT

A DEAD AND STORMY NIGHT

Start the Grimdale Graveyard Mysteries series and dive into a new adventure in the same world as Nevermore Bookshop: http://books2read.com/grimdale1

"Go on, dearie. Let me have a little sniff of that salty goodness."

"No," I snap under my breath as I snatch the pretzels from the tray table and stuff them in my pocket.

For your information, I'm not hanging out in the world's grossest sex club. (That was two years ago in Amsterdam. My shoes stuck to the floor.) I'm sitting in my seat on a flight somewhere over the United Arab Emirates, minding my own business and trying to ignore the ghost of a blue-haired old biddy who is annoyingly fascinated by my airline snacks.

"Pleeeeease? Just hold the bag out so I can have a whiff."

I glare at her before turning my body toward the window. Outside, the world is dark – the kind of deep, unsettling darkness that makes you remember you're hurtling through space at a gazillion miles an hour with only a computer, a hopefully not-drunk pilot, and the laws of physics standing between you and a fiery, dramatic death. We're somewhere over the Middle East, but the cloud cover is so thick that it looks like we're flying into a black hole.

Most people in the cabin are settling down to sleep, but I won't get any peace as long as Chatty Cathy insists on a running commentary of my snacks.

"I know you can see me, dearie," she sighs. I watch out of the corner of my eye as she hovers over the empty seat beside me. "My good friend the headless pilot told me all about you. Well, he didn't tell me so much as gesticulated. He said your thighs were much bigger. You should eat more, put some meat on those bones – starting with those pretzels in your pocket."

I groan. Stupid ghosts. They have no right to be gesticulating about the size of my thighs, which are perfectly fine as they are, thank you very much.

It figures that airplane ghosts talk to each other. There aren't that many of them compared to, say, hospitals, old asylums, and Starbucks stores. They generally stick to the plane where they died but they can hop off at airports and float around in the terminals like some kind of spectral hen party, swapping gossip about their flights. The Headless Pilot and I had a run-in on my flight from Bali last year, and it was not a pleasant experience. I was on the loo, reading a smutty romance novel on my phone and enjoying hour three of *absolutely no dead people* when he stuck his torso through the bathroom door and shook his neck stub at me. I screamed bloody murder because that's what you do when you have a see-through neck stub in your face, and the stewardess had to break down the door because she thought I was having some kind of fit. They didn't believe my story about seeing a spider, and I've been banned from that airline for life.

Ghosts are nothing but trouble.

Usually, airplanes are one of the few places in the world where I'm blissfully free of ghosts for a while. Statistically, not that many people die on planes. It's one of the reasons I decided to leave my small British village of Grimdale the moment I got my GCSE and embark on a backpacking trip around the world. It wasn't the most pressing motivation, but it definitely factored high on my 'reasons to get as far from Grimdale as possible' list.

And now, after all this time, I'm heading *back* to Grimdale, a place I very much do not want to be, because of the terrible thing...

No. I squeeze my eyes shut. *I don't want to think about that. If I burst into tears on this plane, Chatty Cathy will never let me hear the end of it.*

"Excuse me, ma'am?"

I open my eyes and see the reflection of a man in a business suit in the window. Ghosts don't have reflections, so it's a real live person talking to me. That doesn't happen often – my resting bitchface is so legendary that sonnets have been composed in its honor.

I spin around. Businessman McArmaniPants flashes me an apologetic smile. He leans forward and puts his arm on the back of the seat, right through the old lady's spectral head.

"Argh, watch where you're putting those skinbags, you rotten oaf!" She jerks away, holding her head as she hops angrily down the aisle. She looks like a chicken with her bony elbows jerking wildly. I cough into my hand to cover my smirk.

Businessman McArmaniPants flashes me a megawatt smile. "I didn't mean to startle you. I noticed that this seat is empty. I wondered if I could sit next to you – I'm near the back and a kid spilled his orange juice and now everything is sticky—"

"Sure." I pat the seat, grateful for his presence. He'll act as a buffer between me and the old lady ghost. "Please, make yourself at home. Stay as long as you like."

"Do not make yourself at home!" Chatty Cathy huffs, glaring at the man as he lowers himself into her seat. "This is my chair. I claimed it first. Get your own snacks to sniff."

"Do you want some pretzels?" I crack open the bag and offer it to my new seatmate, knowing that the ghost won't want to risk getting close enough to sniff them now.

"Sure." He takes a handful. "Hey, why are you poking out your tongue?"

"Oh." A blush creeps across my cheeks as the old biddy huffs away. "No reason."

Are you ready for a little ghost lore? I'm on the second leg of my thirty-two hours of flying from New Zealand to London, so I have time to kill.

Time to kill. Ha ha. I'm a comedian.

Here's the skinny on the spirits of the dead, aka, Bree's Ghost Rules:

1. Not everyone who dies becomes a ghost. You have to have unfinished business. Often, you don't remember what that business is, which I'm sure must be annoying.

2. Ghosts hang around the location where they died. There's an invisible force I call ghost mojo (it's a highly technical term I came up with when I was eight, shut up) that acts like a rubber band that pulls them back to the location of their death. They can wander away from their death location, but the

ghost mojo gets worse the further they go until it becomes painful for them to remain away and they get sucked back to their death place again.

3. Some ghosts, like my childhood friend Ambrose, aren't tied to a death location but instead, a place that's important to them. I don't know how it works, so I blame it on ghost mojo.

4. Ghost mojo is also why ghosts can fly through airplane bathroom doors but don't fall through the floor and out into space. Ghost mojo keeps spirits standing on the ground the way they did when they were alive.

5. Only very powerful or very angry ghosts can interact with the human world by moving things or flickering lights or writing on mirrors. Mostly they just waft around being annoying.

6. Despite not having noses, they can still sense strong smells, so they're forever lingering around when people are eating and begging to sniff my salty nuts.

7. Ghosts hate it when humans walk through them. *Hate. It.* Sometimes I do it just because I know it pisses them off so much.

How do I know so much about ghosts?

Because I'm the only person who can see them.

I had an accident when I was five years old – I fell off my bike and cracked my head on a rock – and ever since I've been able to see the dead. See them and talk to them and be infinitely harassed by them—

"Go on, dearie," the old lady pokes her head out of the luggage rack. "Just a little sniff."

I'm Bree Mortimer. And it's going to be a long flight.

TO BE CONTINUED

Start reading the Grimdale Graveyard Mysteries series now:
http://books2read.com/grimdale1

OTHER BOOKS BY STEFFANIE HOLMES

Nevermore Bookshop Mysteries

A Dead and Stormy Night

Of Mice and Murder

Pride and Premeditation

How Heathcliff Stole Christmas

Memoirs of a Garroter

Prose and Cons

A Novel Way to Die

Much Ado About Murder

Crime and Publishing

Plot and Bothered

Grimdale Graveyard Mysteries

You're So Dead To Me

If You've Got It, Haunt It

Ghoul as a Cucumber

Not a Mourning Person

Kings of Miskatonic Prep

Shunned

Initiated

Possessed

Ignited

Stonehurst Prep

My Stolen Life

My Secret Heart

My Broken Crown

My Savage Kingdom

Stonehurst Prep Elite

Poison Ivy

Poison Flower

Poison Kiss

Dark Academia

Pretty Girls Make Graves

Brutal Boys Cry Blood

Manderley Academy

Ghosted

Haunted

Spirited

Briarwood Witches

The Castle of Earth and Embers

The Castle of Fire and Fable

The Castle of Water and Woe

The Castle of Wind and Whispers

The Castle of Spirit and Sorrow

Crookshollow Gothic Romance

Art of Cunning (Alex & Ryan)

Art of the Hunt (Alex & Ryan)

Art of Temptation (Alex & Ryan)

The Man in Black (Elinor & Eric)

Watcher (Belinda & Cole)

Reaper (Belinda & Cole)

Wolves of Crookshollow

Digging the Wolf (Anna & Luke)

Writing the Wolf (Rosa & Caleb)

Inking the Wolf (Bianca & Robbie)

Wedding the Wolf (Willow & Irvine)

Want to be informed when the next Steffanie Holmes paranormal romance story goes live? Sign up for the newsletter at www.steffanieholmes.com/ newsletter to get the scoop, and score a free collection of bonus scenes and stories to enjoy!

About the Author

Steffanie Holmes is the *USA Today* bestselling author of kooky, spooky paranormal, cozy fantasy, and gothic romance. Her books feature clever, witty heroines, secret societies, quirky villages where nothing is as it seems, creepy old mansions, and alpha males who *always* get what they want.

Legally-blind since birth, Steffanie received the 2017 Attitude Award for Artistic Achievement. She was also a finalist for a 2018 Women of Influence award.

Steffanie lives in New Zealand with her husband, a horde of cantankerous cats, and their medieval sword collection.

STEFFANIE HOLMES NEWSLETTER

Grab a free copy of *Cabinet of Curiosities* – a Steffanie Holmes compendium of short stories and bonus scenes – when you sign up for updates with the Steffanie Holmes newsletter.

http://www.steffanieholmes.com/newsletter

Come hang with Steffanie
www.steffanieholmes.com
hello@steffanieholmes.com

www.ingramcontent.com/pod-product-compliance
Lightning Source LLC
Chambersburg PA
CBHW032236310726
48973CB00008B/2159